The Age of
Catherine de Medici

*the text of this book is printed
on 100% recycled paper*

The Age of Catherine de Medici

by

J. E. NEALE

Astor Professor of English History in the
University of London

HARPER TORCHBOOKS ❧
The Academy Library
Harper & Row, Publishers
New York

THE AGE OF CATHERINE DE MEDICI. This book was originally published in 1943 by Jonathan Cape Ltd., London, and reprinted in 1945, 1947, 1957, 1959, and 1960. It is here reprinted by arrangement.

Printed in the United States of America

First HARPER TORCHBOOK edition published 1962 by
Harper & Row, Publishers, Incorporated,
New York and Evanston.

CONTENTS

PREFACE   7

I   THE RELIGIOUS BACKGROUND   9

II   THE SOCIAL AND POLITICAL BACKGROUND   33

III   THE MASSACRE OF ST. BARTHOLOMEW   59

IV   THE CLOSE OF THE RELIGIOUS WARS   82

BIBLIOGRAPHICAL NOTE   110

INDEX   113

PREFACE

This book consists of four lectures which were first
written in 1938 and delivered at Alexandra College,
Dublin, in November of that year. They were re-
delivered at the University College of North Wales
in November 1942. Originally, I had no intention of
publishing them, and indeed it is with some diffidence
that I have brought myself to take that step. They are
not the product of research, as scholars use that word,
nor can I claim authority as an expert in French
history. Their justification must be as a short and, I
trust, lucid popularization of a story which is as
dramatic as it is complicated and confusing. I hope
students may find that they smooth what must often
be rough going, and lay readers may be attracted not
only by the intrinsic interest of the story but by the
parallels which it offers with our own day.

J. E. NEALE

University College, London
May 1943

THE RELIGIOUS BACKGROUND

OUR story begins in March 1559 with the Peace of Cateau-Cambrésis. It was primarily a peace between Spain and France, though England too was a party, for Mary Tudor had entered the war in the train of her husband, Philip II, and had lost Calais. This peace marks the close of an epoch in European as well as French history.

The most obvious change in the European scene was its new rulers. Only three to four years before, Philip II had taken over Spain and the Spanish Netherlands from his father, the Emperor Charles V; in England Elizabeth had become Queen the previous November; and in France celebrations connected with the Peace were to result in the death of Henry II and thus lead to the gradual emergence of the Queen-Mother, Catherine de Medici, as the director of French policy. By a striking coincidence all three of these rulers were long-lived. Catherine de Medici died at the turn of the year 1588-89: she was sixty-nine. Philip II died in 1598: he was seventy-one. Elizabeth died in 1603: she was sixty-nine. The second half of the sixteenth century was dominated by these three personalities, and, according to one's national standpoint, is the Age of Philip II, of Elizabeth, or of Catherine de Medici.

The Peace of Cateau-Cambrésis closed the period of the Italian Wars, which had gone on intermittently for over sixty years and ended, from the French point of view, in complete humiliation. France finally gave up the challenge to Spanish hegemony in Italy, and Italy was left to itself and Spain. The Italian states could no longer disturb the peace by playing off one great power against another; they passed out of the main current of international affairs.

The Italian Wars were ended. So also was the second great theme of that period of history — the German Reformation. After years of disorder and civil war, in which the Emperor had tried and failed to accomplish the miracle of uniting rival theologies in a compromise, exhaustion and realism had propounded their own solution — the solution which is described by the Latin tag, *cuius regio eius religio*: the prince determines the faith of his kingdom. The sixteenth century was totalitarian in its political creed: its motto was 'One King, One Faith'. Germany preserved this creed in its Reformation settlement, but paid a heavy price. It shattered itself. The Prince, not the Emperor, was the beneficiary of the German Reformation; and a country which in law was a federal state became in consequence a confederation of states. German unity had to wait until the nineteenth century — or perhaps one should say, until the twentieth. The Reformation settlement was embodied in the Peace of Augsburg in 1555; and thereafter Germany, like Italy, receded from the main current of European affairs and did not re-emerge until the eve of the Thirty Years War, half a century or so later. In that half-century it is western Europe that occupies the stage of history.

Modern research, with its emphasis on economic factors, has a very up-to-date reason for the making of the Peace of Cateau-Cambrésis: money, or rather, the lack of it. Of that I must say a word in a later chapter. But in the mind of the King of France, Henry II, who wanted peace so desperately that he was prepared to surrender almost anything, money was not the only reason. He had an overwhelming desire to tackle a domestic problem, the urgency of which had been growing in recent years. That problem was heresy; and it is the theme of this chapter.

We have all heard, maybe to the point of staleness, about the causes of the Reformation; about the state of the Catholic Church in the early sixteenth century, about worldly and non-resident bishops, ignorant and unspiritual clergy, and the monasteries. The story is the same in France, only perhaps more so, for there, in addition to the general slackness of the age, there was a peculiar reason for the deplorable condition of the Church. It was the Concordat of 1516; an agreement made between the French monarchy and the Papacy, which can only be described as a deal in the spoils of the Gallican Church. It gave the King the nomination to bishoprics, abbeys, and conventual priories in France; and its effect can be put quite briefly. Not a single French bishop obtained his post because of religious zeal or spiritual worthiness. Fifty per cent of benefices were given for Court services, the rest to please influential local magnates; and benefices were actually given to two Italian princes to further French diplomacy in Italy. These appointments were regarded, not as ecclesiastical preferment, but as grants of revenue, a conception that was blatant enough when the grants consisted of all future vacant benefices until their combined revenue should reach a certain sum.

Pluralism was of course scandalous; though it made little odds how many benefices bishops held when they were non-resident. Take as an example the most princely of French churchmen, the Cardinal of Lorraine, who rivalled England's Wolsey in his pluralism. He was Archbishop of Rheims, held the revenues of the bishoprics of Metz and Verdun, and was abbot-in-commendam of eleven abbeys, including the famous abbey of St. Denis which was usually reserved for a member of the royal family. And in addition he controlled an immense amount of ecclesiastical patronage. His income has been estimated at 300,000 *livres* per annum. Most of his appointments were inherited from his uncle — a still greater pluralist — like family estates. He was made Archbishop of Rheims at the age of fourteen, and was a cardinal at twenty-three. He happened to be, in his own way, a rather good churchman; but that fact has the irrelevance of an accident.

Among the lower clergy almost all benefices were part of the patrimony of local families, descending from uncle to nephew, like the Cardinal of Lorraine's holdings. In such circumstances priesthood could not be regarded as a calling, in the evangelical sense: it was merely a qualification to hold a benefice, lightly regarded and lightly conferred. In addition to those with benefices awaiting them, an increasing number of smaller folk took orders as a means of escaping misery and want. They were the hangers-on of the Church, roaming from place to place. Some, by making the highest bid, might farm the benefices of non-resident clergy, and after paying dearly for their posts set about recouping themselves. Pluralism and non-residence were rampant. There were many priests in France, but a wholesale neglect of the spiritual needs of the people. According to a contemporary, there was not one of fifty parishes in Brittany that had its rector resident; while another contemporary, writing from Périgord, declared that near Bordeaux there were forests fifty leagues in extent where the inhabitants lived like beasts of burden, without an idea of heavenly things. There were persons — he went on to say — fifty years of age, who had never heard a Mass nor understood a word of religion. The ignorance, as well as the low spiritual quality of the clergy, was in no small way responsible for this state of affairs. It was said that there was scarcely one priest in ten who was able to read; an estimate which, if inaccurate, was not far wrong. There is little reason to be surprised at the spread of the Reformation in France.

In its early phases the French Reform movement was moderate and respectable. It was the spiritual facet of Humanism, a blending of Erasmian and Lutheran impulses, and had the King's sister for patron. Though admirable in many ways, it lacked the qualities to shape a great rebel cause. Indeed, neither Lutheranism nor Humanism possessed the practical genius required for sustained and successful rebellion. This may seem a strange remark when one thinks of the explosive force of the Lutheran Reformation in Germany: it had been dynamic enough to rouse a whole nation and had accomplished a revolution. But the practical success of the movement had been due to the support of the secular princes. It was they and not Luther who had supplied the Lutheran Church with its organization. Luther was a mystic, not an administrator. To him the Church was not an organized, earthly society, but an invisible body, the mystic communion of saints; and it needed the mundane mind of the Prince to fetch the Church down from the heavens, where Luther had left it suspended, and clothe it in the necessary garments to move about the earth. There were no essential Lutheran doctrines about the form of church organization, and everywhere the Prince supplied that form. Consequently we find the Lutheran Church episcopal in one state and non-episcopal in another.

By the middle of the sixteenth century Lutheranism had lost its revolutionary fervour, become respectable in its dependence upon secular rulers, and shown its essential conservatism, a conservatism reinforced by the worldly timidity of secular policy. The second half of the century was to make this still more evident, for there were times when it seemed as if European Catholicism was uniting in a formidable crusade to smash Protestantism, and attempts were made by Queen Elizabeth and others to form a rival Protestant League. The Lutheran princes met these approaches with fair words but nothing more. Perhaps the wily Elizabeth deserved little else; yet it was all too clear that the crusading spirit had gone out of Lutheranism. If French Protestantism had remained Lutheran it would indeed have been a weak plant.

It would have been weak because in the nature of things the Reformation in France could not count on the support of the King. However much on occasions the French monarchy might seem to wobble, there can be little doubt that it was fated to remain Catholic. What had it to gain from going Reformist? In the all-important business of appointing to bishoprics and wealthy abbeys, the King of France, under the Concordat of 1516, was as much the Head of the Church as Henry VIII of England. A government that was desperately and permanently bankrupt, as France was for the next half-century, that relied on its ecclesiastical patronage to pay officials and courtiers, and that in dire need was able to tax the Church without mercy, could not afford to discard a system which served it so well.

True, the French King might have broken with Rome and, like Henry VIII, become the titular as well as the practical Head of the Church. There was an old and strong tradition of Gallicanism in the French Church, a tradition of national independence which might seem to have suggested a move of this sort; and in the first year or two of our period there actually was an occasional hint to the Papacy that if it did not mind its p's and q's France might follow the example of England. But even if such a change had been practical policy, it would not have satisfied the Reformers. On doctrinal questions a breach with Rome would no doubt have brought some concessions to Protestants, but the last thing the Reformers wanted was the perpetuation of that scandalous laxity and irreligion associated with royal control of the Church. No. The French monarchy was fated to remain Catholic. Its vested interests in the *ancien régime* were too great, and so also were those of powerful elements in the country. Moreover, though Protestant communities developed in Paris and were troublesome, this city was always staunchly, nay fanatically Catholic. It was not an accident that England ultimately took the religious complexion of its capital: London was worth a sermon. Nor was it an accident that France ultimately took the religious complexion of its capital: Paris was worth a Mass.

Thus the French Reform movement, being opposed to the interests of the monarchy, was bound to assume the shape of rebellion. Now, there are certain essentials for prolonged and successful rebellion; and the chief is organization. Here lies the significance of Calvinism. If I am inclined to stress organization over against doctrine or anything else, the reason is my profound conviction of its vital importance. Much of English history, Scottish history, and Dutch history in the second half of the sixteenth century might be written round the organization of Calvinism; and I am often tempted to speak of this period as the Age of Calvin, although in fact Calvin died in 1564.

In Calvin, France produced its own prophet of the Reformation. He fled from his home country in 1534, and did two outstanding things: first, he wrote the bible of the new protestant movement, his *Institution of Christian Religion*, published in Latin in 1536 and afterwards in French and other languages; secondly, he founded at Geneva the Protestants' New Jerusalem, the City of God on earth.

The theological or doctrinal aspect of Calvinism need not detain us. On this subject it is sufficient to note that at a moment when the inherent individualism of the German Reformation was producing confusion in Protestant theology, Calvin, with his legal training and the clarity and rigour of the French genius, rethought Protestant theology into an ordered and logical system. The Gallic qualities of his mind naturally fitted his teaching to become the Protestant gospel of the French people. There was one doctrine of Calvinism — that of predestination, to which Calvin was driven by the relentless logic of his thought — which deserves mention because of its value to a fighting faith. In time of hazard and persecution it was no small fortification to the spirit to know that one was among the elect, predestined by God to salvation.

But it is not the theology, it is the organization of this Church that is the most striking feature in the history of the French Calvinist, or, as it was called, Huguenot movement. Unlike Luther, Calvin did not regard the organization of the Church as a negligible consideration and let the State have its own way. It was an integral part of his teaching. After all, the secret of the power wielded throughout the centuries by the Catholic Church lay in its organization and discipline as well as its dogma. And, as one eminent French historian has put it, Calvin's unique achievement, the sign of his originality, was to construct a new Catholicism outside the old and opposed to it.

This organization, which is better known to most of us by the name Presbyterian, must be examined in some detail. The officers of Calvin's Church were divided into three categories: ministers, elders, and deacons. The elders joined with the ministers in the government and discipline of the Church, while the deacons had charge of the sick and poor. In appearance the scheme had a democratic basis since each minister — and the same was true of elders and deacons — had ultimately to be elected by the particular congregation that he was to serve. But in fact Calvin's Church was oligarchic and conservative. The real choice of candidates for the ministry was in the hands of the body of ministers, who put them through a preliminary and searching examination of their doctrinal views and knowledge of scripture, their preaching ability, and their moral fitness. In Geneva Calvin gave the title of the Venerable Company to his ministers, and he meant them to live up to the title. Discipline was the very essence of his Church, among both officers and rank and file.

Each individual church, in the scheme of ecclesiastical government for countries like France, was governed by its minister and elders, the laity in the persons of the elders joining with the ministry here as throughout the whole organization. Minister and elders together formed a disciplinary committee known as the Consistory, which, by domiciliary visits or otherwise, maintained a constant supervision over the mode of life of every member of the church; an activity which Queen Elizabeth, to whom the Genevan system was anathema, described as an intolerable inquisition to pry into people's lives. This committee might even, and in France did, exercise a minor police power.

Above the Consistory, or ruling body of the single church, was another committee known in France as the Colloquy. It consisted of the ministers and elders of a number of neighbouring churches, grouped into a district, over which they exercised a general supervision, dealing with business brought to them by the individual churches. Above the Colloquy was the Synod, also a governing body of ministers and elders. In a large country like France there would be Provincial Synods, and, capping the whole ecclesiastical organization, a National Synod.

Think what this organization meant; think, especially, how well it was adapted to the cause of rebellion. Isolation, which breeds fear, doubt, and surrender in all but the most courageous, was impossible. No sooner was a community formed than it was organized; no sooner were there several communities than they were linked together by the Colloquy; and on top of this came the Provincial Synod and finally the National Synod to weld all the churches into a single unit.

Throughout every grade of this organization ran the remarkable Calvinist discipline, which maintained unity of belief and a high code of personal conduct. At the meetings of each governing committee there were always two items of procedure in addition to business matters: an exposition of some passage of the Bible, and what was called a censure. In Colloquy and Synod a different minister undertook the biblical exposition at each meeting, and when he had finished, his colleagues proceeded to criticize. Two important objects were achieved by these scriptural exercises: first, uniformity of doctrine — and the Bible was there on the table, as at all Calvinist meetings, the ultimate authority of the Church in case of disagreement; and secondly, a decent level of preaching ability, no small matter in that sermonless age.

At the conclusion of meetings, whether of Consistory, Colloquy, or Synod, there took place an 'amicable and brotherly censure', in which those present reviewed each other's conduct and life, offering friendly criticism. It may strike us as a humourless procedure, and we may wonder how much 'amicable censure' brotherly feeling could really stand. But we must not forget the appalling spiritual and moral laxity of the age, against which it was a reaction; nor should we forget that the totalitarian states of our own day, which in some respects Calvin's Geneva resembled, intrude into the private lives of citizens with their party discipline. The discipline had more than its ordinary value in France, for, as we shall see, in the early days of the Huguenot movement congregations had often to meet at night. As Calvinism had thrown over the Catholic doctrine of salvation by works, its adherents easily laid themselves open to a charge of libertinism, and these secret night-meetings were liable to provoke much the same slander as was levelled against the early Christians.

Here are some examples of censures from French Consistories: M. Manget, the preacher, was told that he did not preach popularly enough and repeated himself too much; another minister was told not to preach so quickly. As for laymen: M. Rozel was urged to go to the sermon more frequently, manage the maids in his house better, and be less ready to air his opinions; another was censured for avarice; another for lending money at usury; another for ill-treating his wife; another for playing piquet; others for dancing and drinking. Though severe, the discipline was beneficial in its results. In France the Consistory often acted like Justices of the Peace and stopped much useless litigation in a litigious age. Morals were reformed, a purposeful and industrious way of life encouraged, and material prosperity followed in the wake of godliness. In the words of Tyndale's Translation: 'The Lorde was with Joseph, and he was a luckie felowe.'

So much for the organization and discipline of the

Calvinist Church. We must next see how Calvin meant his Church to fit into the State. Once more he was precise and logical. State and Church were separate powers, but they were fused, first by the assumption that every citizen would be a member of the Church, and secondly by the unique position accorded to the Bible. Calvin regarded the Bible as the word of God, in the full and literal sense. Consequently, in a godly society it should be the fundamental law both of the State and the Church. Now the Bible is full of moral injunctions, and the Old Testament in particular, with its Mosaic laws, embodies a whole penal code. These injunctions and this code, being the word of God, should therefore be part of the law of the State: for example, death is the punishment for adultery in the Old Testament, and it should be the same in the Calvinist State. From our point of view the conception reveals a monstrous confusion of morality and law; the sort of confusion which, in a minor degree perhaps, the contemporary totalitarian State has made. But it is not my object to condemn or praise; and I hasten to make a final point about Calvin's State. It is this: since the Bible was to be the fundamental law of the State, and since the professional expositors of the Bible were the ministers, it followed that the ministers would in fact dominate State as well as Church. In other words, Calvin's State would be a theocracy; a natural conclusion, for he drew his inspiration from the Old Testament and the Israelitish theocracy.

This in brief was Calvin's theory of Church and State — his vision of Utopia. In the course of the centuries many authors have written Utopias; few indeed have had the opportunity and the ideal conditions for putting them to the actual experiment. This perfect and rarest of Fortune's gifts was Calvin's. Geneva became his theocracy. It would involve me in unpardonable irrelevance if I stopped to explain how that city came to be the ideal laboratory for his ideas. I can only say that a theocracy, more or less as Calvin planned, was established there.

That simple fact is of profound importance. We ourselves have seen and still see, in the recent past and the present, the infectious character of ideas translated into political institutions. Communist and Fascist states have shaken the world by the enthusiasm they have aroused in other countries; and also, it must be added, by the detestation. The same contagious emotional quality belonged to Calvin's Geneva. To puritans in every land it represented the New Jerusalem, the godly society in actual working order; a demonstration that their dreams were realizable. The missionary value of this model state can hardly be exaggerated. Making allowance for the differing scale of the world, its influence was perhaps more formidable than that of Communist Russia in our own day.

Moreover, Geneva was a small state, standing outside the system of great nation-states and therefore well suited to be the centre of an international movement. In this it was like Rome, its religious rival; but with a difference that was to Geneva's advantage, for by long tradition Rome was also a centre of national diplomacies and its prestige as a spiritual metropolis suffered from the notorious and very unspiritual clash of national interests there.

The metropolitan character of Geneva was revealed

in many ways. Its school and university became international institutions, attaining the fame and more than the influence of Wittenberg under Luther and Melancthon. It became the training college of ministers, especially for France. And the correspondence that Calvin carried on, immense in volume and international in scope, was perhaps the most remarkable personal correspondence of the age.

As wave after wave of religious exiles fled now from this country and now from that, Geneva took on the role of a city of refuge. Many English protestants fled there in Mary Tudor's reign; and as the French religious troubles developed, the city was overwhelmed by Huguenot refugees and was subject to an almost unbearable strain. Here are some figures that give an idea of the increasing influx of refugees. They are from the registers of new inhabitants, and show, in 1549 eighty-one; in 1550, one hundred and forty-five; in 1551, two hundred and sixty-four; in 1557, five hundred and eighty-seven; and Geneva, let us remember, was only a small city-state. A letter in December 1572 gives some idea of the refugee problem after the Massacre of St. Bartholomew, which had taken place in the previous August. There were, the letter says, more than seven hundred people in the city ordinarily needing assistance; and this figure did not include a great number employed on public works, who for the moment, but for the moment only, could support themselves; nor did it include those passing through the city and requiring help *en route*; while there were also fifty refugee ministers, all poor. The parallel with our own times will be obvious. Paris, into which Russian, Italian, German, and Austrian political refugees were pouring between 1918 and 1939, has perhaps in this respect been most like Calvinist Geneva.

It was from Geneva that the French Huguenot movement was organized. From here and neighbouring Protestant cities, Protestant literature was carried secretly through France by colporteurs and distributed surreptitiously by booksellers. It is significant that between 1549 and 1557 no less than fifty-six printers and booksellers sought refuge in Geneva. From here also missionaries went forth. As Huguenot congregations were formed it was to Geneva that they applied for ministers, and it was there that they sent their young men to be trained for the ministry. On questions of government and policy they were continually writing to Calvin. Once more I think that a contemporary parallel may be helpful. Calvin's Geneva was in many ways like Moscow during those years after the war of 1914-1918 when the Soviet State dreamed of a world communist revolution: it was as much a thorn in the side of the French government as Moscow in the side of capitalist Germany before 1933.

Though this account of Calvin and Geneva has not, I hope, exceeded the length that their place in French history warrants, it is time that we examined the growth of the Calvinist movement in France itself.

First, let us look at the classes of people who responded to Reformist propaganda. We can best begin with the one class that it scarcely touched — the peasantry. With certain exceptions they were hostile. They were completely illiterate and thus could not be affected by the clandestine literature that played so large a part in Huguenot propaganda; and as was inevitable with people rooted to the soil, they were profoundly conservative. They were attached to the worship of saints and the cult of the dead; and it was only when Reformist ideas began to grip the nobility and gentry that any of them were won over to the cause, and then by tenant-loyalty rather than religious conversion.

As might be expected, it was among the educated, at the universities, that the new doctrine spread first. Many university teachers and also tutors in noble households were converted, and in due course influenced the minds of their pupils. Medical men, lawyers, and notaries, and other professional men figured prominently in Huguenot ranks. The lawyer class in France was very large and, in comparison with the less bureaucratic government of England, was used in great numbers in the administration of the country. They formed almost an estate in themselves, and their traditions were anti-clerical. It was generally from the rank and file of the profession that Huguenot converts were obtained. They played an important part in the movement, for they were able secretly to shelter heretics from the operation of the laws against them.

These professional men were mostly the sons of merchants, whose trade connections with other countries brought them into touch with new-fangled ideas, and who, by their independent spirit and quality of mind, as a class were everywhere inclined to anticlericalism and heresy. In France they had additional cause for discontent in the grave financial drain caused by the Italian Wars. Their professional sons had no small part in converting them to Calvinism; and the organization of the Huguenot Church, by providing through the offices of elders and deacons for bourgeois laity in church government, appealed to their *amour-*

propre. The spirit of Calvinism was, as I have said, essentially oligarchic and bourgeois.

Among the clergy, the bishops kept more or less clear of the infection. Only four went over to Geneva; five more were restless. Otherwise, in contrast with the English Reformation, the episcopacy was the great obstacle to heresy. It was the lower clergy and especially the Friars who became Huguenots. For three centuries the Friars had been the militia of the Church. They thronged the universities, and by their preaching, their mysticism, and their contacts with the people, were the true leaders of the crowd. They were a great asset and a great nuisance: speculators in doctrine and rebels against discipline, their tradition was one of independence and turbulence. They proved readily accessible to Genevan ideas, and were invaluable in the early stages of the Reform movement as peripatetic preachers of heresy, profiting by the non-residence of bishops and the immunities of their orders to overrun the country. They provided the new Church in France with its first ministers. But their indiscipline and their democratic spirit, both of which Calvin loathed, detracted from their service. One of Calvin's correspondents described them as 'these horrible beasts'; and Calvin himself was far from enamoured of such turbulent pioneers.

The nobility — a class which included what we in England would term the country gentry — was the last class to be won over in large numbers. Very few were Calvinists in 1547, but twelve years later the situation had changed remarkably. Education and the influence of their women-folk were important factors in their conversion. With the women it was religious feeling — a revulsion against the moral and religious laxity of Francis I's reign; but with their men-folk the motive was often revolt against a social and political regime of which they were the victims. Moreover, they had lost a good deal by the Concordat of 1516, before which they had been able to secure high ecclesiastical positions for their sons. They tended to be anti-clerical and anticipated spoils for themselves in the form of Church lands if the Reform movement triumphed.

The recruiting of the lesser nobility — the country gentry — was of great practical service. They might be described as the Storm-Troopers of the Huguenot movement. As a class they were entitled and accustomed to carry swords, and they therefore constituted a natural protection for meetings of heretic congregations. There was need for this. At first Huguenot congregations met in secret and often at night, in cellars or in the countryside outside the towns. Their meetings were illegal and liable to be broken up by the authorities. A more frequent danger was attack by hostile bands of Catholics, for, as the movement spread, it inflamed passions, as the growth of the Nazi movement did in Germany; and just as there were incessant clashes and fights between Communists and Nazis in the days before Hitler succeeded to power, so there were clashes and fights between Catholics and Huguenots. The gentry were needed to protect the Huguenot ministers and their flocks from assault, and congregations often met with a body of armed protectors forming a circle of defence round them. The churches came to place themselves, each under some nobleman as their protector.

As the number of converts increased, the situation

deteriorated, breeding further aggression on both sides, for there were few ministers available in the earlier stages of the movement and congregations were therefore apt to grow so large that they were forced to meet in public. Secrecy was no longer possible. An extract from the minutes of the Consistory of Mans, dated August 6th, 1561, illustrates this transition to public meetings: 'It has been decided that M. Merlin shall commence to preach publicly under the town hall of this town on Sunday next at 7.0 a.m. Superintendents will make haste to warn faithful noblemen (*gentilshommes*) so that all the faithful of this town shall be at the meeting.' After this beginning, the minister at Mans preached in public four times a week.

Naturally, when secret meetings gave place to public, ministers were no longer able to exercise adequate control over the recruiting of their audiences, and rowdy elements appeared, only too ready to start image-breaking. Moreover, there was an impulse, which the ministers could not well restrain, to seize buildings, especially churches, for Huguenot services. This was often done in a hot-headed and riotous way. In Languedoc and Guienne bands of fanatics drove priests and worshippers out of churches and attacked convents. Similar happenings took place in other parts of the country, though occasionally, where Catholics were lukewarm, amicable arrangements were made with them and churches were shared between the new and the old faiths.

The change from secret to open worship — a significant stage in the Huguenot story — took place during the years 1560 and 1561. Disorder spread through France. Where Catholics were in a majority they turned on the Huguenots and engaged in bloody strife; where the Huguenots were strong, extremists often got out of hand and terrorized the Catholics.

Speaking in general terms — for it would be wearisome, and not very illuminating, to discuss the question in detail, province by province — the Huguenot movement tended to be strong in centres of international trade; for example, at Lyons, the great entrepôt near to the Genevan and German centres of Protestantism, and in the east in Brittany where trade connections with England and the Netherlands encouraged its growth. Normandy too was badly infected with heresy, though here the chief inducement was social and political discontent among the gentry of a province where the evils of French government were exceptionally rife. The movement also flourished in the south, from the Rhône and Provence through Languedoc to the King of Navarre's territory in the south-west. Paris had heretics, but remained predominantly and fervently Catholic: the Huguenot stronghold over against Catholic Paris was Orleans, where some idea of the numbers may be gathered from the fact that in May 1561 five to six thousand persons attended Communion and more than ten thousand followed Protestant funerals. In May 1561 there were said to be two thousand one hundred and fifty separate Huguenot churches in France.

The important years for the organization of the Church were 1555 to 1559. Since 1555 the separate churches had been organizing themselves, largely under the influence and direction of Calvin, who wanted to put a stop to disorder and establish a responsible ministry and proper discipline. Then in

May 1559 the first National Synod was held in Paris. The meeting was in a lodging house, so that the coming and going would not attract attention; and the number present may have reached fifty. They were obscure men, for as yet the nobility had not imposed itself upon the leadership of the Church; and all of them risked death by their presence. They drew up a confession of faith and articles of discipline, including a constitution or organization for the whole Church.

Orderly development upon a settled model could now go forward. That model I have already described. At the base was the Consistory, the governing body of the single church, comprising the minister and lay elders. Its meetings were frequent, sometimes every fortnight. Next there was the Colloquy, the assembly for the combined churches of a district, meeting from twice to four times a year. Then came the Provincial Synod, the province coinciding with the political divisions of France: the number of such Synods was fifteen or sixteen, and they met once or twice a year. Finally there was the National Synod, consisting of two ministers and two elders from each province. It was supposed to meet once a year, and, in accordance with Calvin's insistence on equality among both ministers and churches — a deliberate reaction against the primacy of Rome and the hierarchy of the Catholic Church — to meet at a different town on each occasion. Actually, there were sixteen National Synods between 1559 and 1601, which, considering the chronic state of civil war, was a striking sign of the vitality of this, the supreme governing body of the Huguenot Church.

Such an organization — the organization of a rebel movement within the State — would be remarkable at any time in any State. It is nothing short of astounding to find it within the sixteenth-century State.

That is not all. I have already noted how the nobility, when they joined the movement, naturally took over the protection of congregations. During the turbulent years 1560 and 1561 most of the individual churches placed themselves under a noble protector. Consistories and Synods encouraged this, and the nobility took their place, by right of birth, on the governing bodies of the churches they protected.

The dangerous possibilities of this development were soon evident. The French nobility still retained the old feudal traditions which grouped the lesser nobles under the leadership of greater noblemen, and these in turn under still greater, until the few greatest noblemen in the land were reached — a feudal pyramid. Obviously, this grouping of the nobility fitted perfectly into the pyramid organization of the Huguenot Church, with its district, provincial, and national bodies. And so the Church was able and indeed tempted to create a military organization coinciding with its ecclesiastical organization. The individual church had its captain, the Colloquy its colonel, and the Province its general (*chef-général*). This was the military organization devised in November 1561 for the provinces of Bordeaux and Toulouse.

At this point I can, for the moment, leave my story, for I am verging on the political problem of the age — the subject of my next chapter. I would merely ask you to consider the amazing character and terrifying possibilities of this organized heretical party; consider also the passions that its growth had aroused in France. And I know no better way to secure an imaginative grasp of the situation than to reflect on the turbulent history of the ideological movements in our own days — the history of the Fascist movement in Italy, and better still of the Nazi movement in Germany. Governments have collapsed before them.

THE SOCIAL AND POLITICAL
BACKGROUND

EARLIER in this narrative I said that modern research
has a very up-to-date reason for the making of the
Peace of Cateau-Cambrésis: money. We may take this
as the starting point for examining the condition in
which the long period of the Italian Wars, and their
last phase in particular, had left France. For some time
— in fact, since the reign of that extravagant and pic-
turesque king, Francis I — war had become ruinously
expensive. Henry VIII of England had discovered
this in the latter years of his reign, and, although he
had the wealth of the monasteries on which to fall
back, his by-no-means spectacular military adventures
undermined English government finance. It was the
misfortune of Europe, and especially of Spain and
France, that the disastrous business of war, with its
new and costly methods, could go on because international business and credit were just developing on a
modern scale and could be made the means by which
kings might impoverish their own and other countries.
As yet the evil of credit inflation had not been realized,
and bankers and others were therefore the easy victims
of a royal rake's progress.

Now it so happens — and this is significant for our
study of the Age of Catherine de Medici — that the
first great credit inflation of modern times, with its
nemesis of state bankruptcy, took place in the years

1557 and 1558, setting in motion a series of financial crises that were to last through the rest of the century and on into the next. This inflation was the result of the last phases of the war between France and Spain. Both countries had needed very large sums of money — far beyond their immediate or, with safety, their prospective revenues — to carry on the war. And both countries had developed the instrument of credit. They had established what we term funded debts — permanent state loans, the interest on which formed annuities for those investing in them. The French call these *rentes*, and quite small people had their savings invested in them in the sixteenth century as to-day. The *rentier* class in France had been in existence and had been growing since the 1520s.

However, the main monetary resources for war came, not from permanent but from short-term loans, raised by the French king mainly at the great banking centre of Lyons, and by the Spanish king at Antwerp. At first these loans had been regarded by individual bankers with suspicion, but the habit of making them grew, and as the interest that kings were ready to pay increased to twelve per cent and then sixteen per cent, the prospect of a fine bargain broke down restraint. In 1555 Henry II of France carried through a transaction, the name of which we may translate as the Great Deal. He renewed his immense loans at Lyons, some of which had been at twelve per cent interest, contracted new loans, and put both old and new on a sixteen per cent interest basis. The transaction created a kind of South Sea Bubble. Everyone rushed to share in the Deal, layman and professional, widow and merchant, prince and gentleman, French, Swiss, German, even the Turk.

At the same time Philip II of Spain was working the money market at Antwerp for all that he was worth, or rather, for a great deal more. Both kings had outrun their resources, though their war needs were by no means satisfied. Nemesis followed. In 1557 Philip went bankrupt. Henry II managed to fool his creditors for a few months by asserting that the King of France would not break his word; and oddly enough there were people ready to believe him. Then he too defaulted. The credit inflation burst; and to put it rather crudely both kings had to make peace because wars then as now were fought on paper — paper-credit — and supplies had disappeared.

Financial stability is of course one of the main sources of the strength of a state; and here was the French State about to enter a critical period in its history with its credit ruined and colossal debts. The debt at the death of Henry II was over forty million *livres*; the royal income then, much of which never reached the Treasury, was approximately twelve million. The *livre* equalled about two shillings of contemporary English money, and perhaps some idea of the meaning of these sums may be obtained by remembering that Queen Elizabeth's annual revenue at the beginning of her reign averaged little more than a quarter of a million pounds.

A desperate budgetary position was not the only lamentable consequence of the war period. Naturally enough, the French monarchy had exploited taxation as well as other devices for raising revenue, to their extreme limits; and these limits, it is worth noting, were much greater than in England, where direct taxation could only be levied through parliament.

The French king could tax on his own authority. So heavy, in fact, did the main direct tax — the *taille* — become that peasants left their lands and fled from it. There were certain sections of the country, of which Normandy was an example, where for various reasons the exactions and abuses of the government could go further than elsewhere; and these provinces readily lent themselves to Huguenot propaganda. Generally speaking, social discontent found an outlet for itself in religious and political unrest.

The machinery of government itself suffered from the financial straits of the monarchy. French local government was already very different from that in England, which remained in the unpaid hands of the landed gentry; and while the rapid increase of governmental activity associated with the rise of the modern state was accompanied by a remarkable expansion of the administrative duties of the English gentry as Justices of the Peace, in France the nobility or landed gentry were stripped of their feudal share in the government of the country, and more and more the business of local government, like that of central government, was placed in the hands of lawyer-officials of the State. This growing bureaucracy ought to have been a source of strength to the French monarchy, to which the professional administrator owed office, salary, and career. But in its overwhelming need for money, the Crown had taken a page out of the Papacy's book and had recourse to the sale of offices: officials were compelled to purchase their posts. Control was inevitably sacrificed, for a bureaucracy cannot be disciplined without the right of dismissal, and this had virtually gone. Thus when the severe trial of civil war fell on the French monarchy, one of the chief means of governing was deficient.

The mere sale of offices was not all; for Henry II, again like the Papacy, had taken to the creation of new offices and the multiplication of old, not because the administration required an increase of officials, but because the Crown needed ready money for new wars and could obtain it in this way. The policy was hopelessly short-sighted. Salaries were small, yet were often not paid. In 1559 the whole royal pay-roll, from high officials to common soldiers, was badly in arrears, in many instances for years. Officials had to recoup themselves from the wretched people who came under their charge or needed to use their services. And thus to the crippling burden of taxation was added the vexatious weight of official exactions.

Another element of weakness was the state of the lesser nobility or country gentlemen. As a class they were vulnerable at two points where the English gentry were protected. In the first place, the system of entail of estates, with descent to the eldest son only — a system which, whatever its injustice, has the advantage of preserving the wealth and standing of a family through generations — was not rigorously applied. Estates were constantly being broken up and the wealth of the main line of a noble house diminished. Secondly, in the sixteenth century a final ban was placed on the entry of French noblemen and their children into trade. In contrast with the custom of England, all the sons of the nobility were noble. They were thus precluded from that salutary participation in commerce which refreshed the wealth of the English gentry. For the younger sons of the gentry, cursed with the empty dignity of nobility, war was the only career; and as that career was closed by the termination of the Italian Wars in 1559 they were left without employment. And to make matters worse, they had latterly been fighting without pay since the royal Treasury was empty.

The lesser nobility in 1559 were in a very bad way. Their social functions had largely gone with the transfer of local government from them to lawyer-bureaucrats. They were immune in theory from the main tax, the *taille*; but in practice this was not entirely true, and in any case they had to bear an appreciable part of the financial burden. They had been compelled to contribute to forced loans; they had been victims of the great speculation in royal loans at luring but unpaid interest; in 1555 they had been cruelly hit by a heavy royal levy of money. And they found themselves in a ruinous age. Their rank compelled them to spend money on the education of their children and burdened them with the growing luxury in dress and display, while the great price-revolution in the second half of the sixteenth century, which caused a slump in the value of money at least as drastic as that in our own lifetime since 1914, played havoc with their finances, since rentals tended to remain fixed. Last blow of all, peace brought an end to their career of war.

They raised mortgages, they went bankrupt. And as in England in the sixteenth century, though to a far greater extent, they saw merchants and the lawyer-sons of merchants ousting them from their estates, becoming country gentry, and receiving patents of nobility. Some noblemen in desperation took to brigandage, forming those bands of marauders who were recruited for the Conspiracy of Amboise and were later to help in making the Religious Wars scenes of murder and rapine.

The picture which I have drawn is that of a country needing above all things a period of peace, firm government, and retrenchment. This was not to be. In June 1559, during a tilt at celebrations connected with the Peace of Cateau-Cambrésis, the King, Henry II, whose folly and prodigality had brought France to the verge of ruin, was mortally wounded. He left a family of four boys, the eldest of whom and the successor to the throne, Francis II, was only fifteen.

In the New Monarchies of the sixteenth century, government was essentially personal. Its whole mechanism, from the core of councillors whom the King chose to advise him, reflected the personality of the monarch. Loyalty was a personal feeling towards the King, not towards the abstraction of the State; and the secret of successful government was that power should rest on this loyalty and both be merged in the Crown. Obviously, a boy could be no more than the titular repository of power. The reality must be somewhere else. Consequently, power was bound to become an object of competition among the various claimants to it at Court.

England under Edward VI demonstrated this sixteenth-century truth; and the rivalry of the great lords, Somerset and Northumberland, for the control of power is one of the notorious passages of our history. Who, then, were the Somersets and Northumberlands of France? Who were the leading personalities at Court and what Court parties were there at this time?

The answer must begin with the Queen-Mother, Catherine de Medici. She was just forty years old at the death of her husband, Henry II. She was a daughter of the Medici, the ruling House of Florence, and niece of the Medici Pope Clement VII. Her marriage at the age of fourteen and a half to Henry, then only the second son of Francis I and unlikely to succeed to the throne, had been a move in Francis I's Italian diplomacy. It was a *mésalliance*: indeed, how else could the marriage of a French king's son to the daughter of an Italian merchant family — for that was the origin of the Medici — be regarded? But it was to be justified by Papal policy. Unfortunately Pope Clement died in less than a year, and the justification did not mature. Then, the death of the Dauphin made Henry the heir to the throne, thus aggravating the blunder of the marriage; and, final catastrophe, for seven years Catherine remained childless. For a time there was talk of repudiating her, and, no doubt, if she had continued childless we should have had a 'divorce' that might have helped to make the marital adventures of Henry VIII of England a little more understandable to modern writers. The situation called for all Catherine's skill and sweetness to postpone a decision. Children alone could save her. And at last they came. In rapid succession she bore ten. The danger was past.

Life with her husband, while not so total an eclipse as has often been said, needed much tact, for Henry II was dominated by his mistress, the notorious Diane de Poitiers, who though twenty years older than himself managed to maintain her hold on him till the last. It says much for Catherine that she tolerated this situation, without loss of dignity and without forfeiting her husband's respect. It says still more for her that when her chance came of revenge, which everyone expected and which the mercenary nature of Diane would have justified, she was content merely to dismiss the woman from Court and make her surrender the jewels that she had acquired.

A fairly stern school of experience: life had certainly been that for Catherine. She never overcame the sense of her inferior origin, and her exaggerated respect for royalty was time and again to influence her policy. She pursued crowns for her children as wealthy American matrons — according to repute — once pursued titled husbands for their daughters. She was not an intellectual, nor was she genuinely cultured, but as a true daughter of the Italian Renaissance she liked to patronize the arts and have the trappings of culture about her. She had a live sense of the splendour of royalty, derived from the extravagant Court of her father-in-law, Francis I, and, being a very rich woman in her private fortune, she indulged her taste for showiness and was insatiate in her love of building. Her reckless extravagance in the midst of the terrible financial distress of her country is not a pleasing aspect of her character.

She was undoubtedly a woman of great qualities, if not a great woman. Her vitality was boundless: she was always ready, with tireless energy, to tackle every difficulty that arose. But she lacked any grasp of principles, and was apt to see political problems in terms of a Palace intrigue which could be solved by getting folk together and making them shake hands. She was, in fact, a politician, a very able politician, not a statesman; and her charm coupled with her vitality made her most successful at the game.

Modern psychologists would shake their heads over her possessive maternalism. She loved her children and dominated them with her affection and personality in a way that was ruinous to them. The blackest event in her whole story — the Massacre of St. Bartholomew — had its root in this instinct. To a certain extent it was her desire to mother her children that led her to desire the regency of France, though once she had tasted political power her energy led her to guard and monopolize it with passion.

Among the high nobility at Court there were three parties. The first was that of the Bourbons, who were princes of the blood, heirs to the throne should the reigning House of Valois die out. Their head was Anthony of Navarre, who had married the Queen of that small state, situated in the south-west corner of France. He was a wretched specimen of a leader, fickle, shifty, backboneless, easily twisted round Catherine de Medici's little finger; and characteristically his one ambition in life was to get back the portion of his kingdom of Navarre that Spain had conquered. It was always possible to divert his attention from French politics by talk of inducing Philip II to restore his lost territories, a prospect the utter hopelessness of which he ought to have had the wit to see. When he was mortally wounded in the first Religious War his death removed a futile personality.

The real leader of the Bourbons was Anthony's younger brother, Louis, Prince of Condé. Here was the true figure of a faction-leader; a brave fighter, a good companion, but a hot-headed, restless, ambitious person who in a struggle for power would inevitably assert the claims of his family, as princes of the blood, to the first place at Court.

The second party was that of the Guise family. They

were a younger branch of the House of Lorraine, and therefore half foreign; but it had been the policy of Francis I and Henry II to neglect the princes of the blood and raise this foreign family, along witn certain of the French nobility, to the dignity of dukes and peers, ranking in all but blood with the princes. The Guise family had profited enormously from the favour of Francis I: its lands were immense and so were its ecclesiastical holdings. Moreover, the Duke of Guise was allied by marriage to the French monarchy, while Mary of Guise was Queen-Mother of Scotland and Regent for her daughter, Mary Queen of Scots, whom the Guise by a brilliant coup had married to the Dauphin of France, now the new King, Francis II. They talked of being descended from Charlemagne; and had the two leading members of the House, the Duke of Guise and the Cardinal of Lorraine, not been such attractive personalities, their pride would have been insufferable. They pretended to a place in the Kingdom, lower of course than the King but above everyone else, even the princes of the blood. Frenchmen distrusted their ambition and their foreign strain.

Francis, Duke of Guise, was a brilliant soldier, with the laurels of Calais, which he had taken from the English in 1558, still fresh on his brow. Charles, Cardinal of Lorraine, his brother, was the wealthiest ecclesiastic in France, a highly-cultured churchman, an eloquent preacher, and the statesman of the family.

The third great family was the Montmorency. Its head was the Constable, Anne de Montmorency, the supreme military officer of France. He had been raised to high favour by Francis I, and then, after an eclipse, had returned to power under Henry II. He owed his

43

position and wealth to the monarchy, and Henry II's dependence on him as his chief minister had been constant. But the Guise family had always been present to play the role of rivals, and the last phase of the Italian Wars had not only been a triumph for Guise war policy over the Constable's counsel of peace, it had also seen the Constable defeated and taken prisoner at St. Quentin — a striking disaster for French arms — while the saviour of the country had been the Duke of Guise, victor of Calais. The Montmorency accordingly had good reason to hate the Guise, and they hated them no less because their own tradition, in contrast with Guise ambition, was one of inflexible loyalty to the Crown.

The Constable had three nephews. Unlike their uncle, whose orthodoxy was as unswerving as his loyalty, they were all converted to the Huguenot faith. The eldest of the three was Gaspard de Coligny, the Admiral of France. He inherited all the fine qualities of the family. His conversion was a genuine act of faith, not a move in factional strife or personal ambition; and in the whole sordid story of the Religious Wars he is the one great leader who stands out as the man without reproach.

These three leading families practically divided France between them. Through a system of patronage and clientage, there was scarcely a nobleman, great or small, who was not attached, directly or indirectly, to one or other of them. The lands and influence of the Guise family, the largest of the three, covered the whole eastern provinces of the realm; those of the Bourbons covered the west; and the Montmorency held sway in the centre.

As Guise and Bourbon each claimed priority of the other at Court, it was impossible for the monarchy to satisfy both at the same time; and the situation, disconcerting enough in itself, had by 1559 become dangerous when this clash of political ambitions aligned itself with the religious divisions of the country.

Condé was converted to the Huguenot faith in 1558, though indeed religion sat lightly on him and he exercised a prince's licence in his private life that would have shocked Calvin. He naturally assumed the military leadership of the Huguenots when that aspect of their movement revealed and developed itself in the next two or three years, thus becoming their evil genius, for his inclinations and his rank as a prince of the blood lent impetus and respectability to all aggressive impulses. Anthony of Navarre, the head of the Bourbons, was also a Huguenot. But in religion as in everything else he was spineless: it was his wife, a woman of great force of character and an ardent Protestant, who had converted him.

With the Bourbons now at the head of Protestantism, the Guise naturally assumed the leadership of the Catholics. The Montmorency, however, remained divided. The Constable was not to be divorced from his faith, nor his nephews from theirs. Creed in this instance was stronger than family; a new phenomenon in French history, and one which increased the difficulties of the French government, for the obvious way of maintaining political equilibrium was dependence on the Montmorency in alliance with one of the other two parties, thus keeping the third party under control.

A final point. All these men, who were to play a prominent part in the opening phases of the Religious Wars, were, with the exception of the Constable, young, or at any rate not old, men. The Duke of Guise was forty in 1559, the Cardinal of Lorraine thirty-four, Anthony of Navarre forty-one, Condé twenty-nine, and Coligny forty-one. Their lieutenants were younger: all less than thirty. And young men are not servants of tranquillity.

Though technically of age, Francis II was only fifteen and a half when he succeeded to the throne in 1559, and it was obvious that there would have to be a regency, in fact if not in name. This was the opportunity of the Guise family. Through their niece, the new Queen, Mary of Scots, Francis was persuaded to place himself and the government of his country in their hands. They made friendly advances to Catherine de Medici, and found her ready to acquiesce in the situation. France passed under Guise control.

Their task was an unenviable one. The end of the Italian Wars — as we have seen — had brought an insoluble financial problem, failure to meet debts, widespread social distress, the dismissal of soldiers who had not received their pay. The odium of it all descended on the Guise, and stuck more easily because there was the taint of the foreign adventurer about them and their personal ambition was thought to be limitless. Then, too, the religious problem had reached a crisis. This they tried to solve by continuing with increased energy Henry II's savage policy of persecution, thus adding to their unpopularity and piling on themselves the hatred of the Huguenot party.

The way was no smoother at Court. The restless Condé had seen, in the accession of a boy to the throne, the chance of making the political fortunes of himself and his family. The King, he contended, was legally still a minor, a Regent ought therefore to be appointed, and by the constitution of France one person and one only had the right to that post — the first prince of the blood, Anthony of Navarre. In his eyes the Guise brothers were mere usurpers of power, who, by the device of proclaiming the King of age, had evaded the necessity of appointing a Regent and so had excluded Condé's brother from the government of the country.

With much persuasion Condé induced his brother to come to Court to claim his rights; but when he arrived, Anthony's nerve failed him and he returned to his estates without playing the game that had been planned. As Condé could make no constitutional claim in his own name, he was left, after his brother's defection, with the alternative of acquiescing in Guise rule or turning to conspiracy. He chose conspiracy.

This was the origin of the Conspiracy of Amboise, the first outward sign of that civil strife towards which France was drifting. The Conspiracy was talked of as early as September 1559; and gradually preparations spread throughout the country. The nominal leader was a member of the lesser nobility named La Renaudie, but the real head was Condé, the 'silent chief', that mysterious great lord of whom the government heard and whose identity they could easily guess, though they were unable to secure adequate proof of his responsibility. The conspirators' plan was for a small group to make their way into the royal palace while the Court was at Amboise in March 1560, and seize the King and the Guise brothers, killing the latter if they resisted. This palace revolution was to be consolidated by the support of a large army which was to arrive at Amboise in small bands from all over

France and hide in the woods till the signal was given. Captains were to be stationed in the principal towns of the country to stir up trouble and so prevent the passage of troops going to the aid of the government. Once the Guise had been seized, Condé was to arrive at Court, voice the country's grievances to King and Council, and secure the punishment of his rivals.

The Conspiracy was prepared by widespread propaganda, especially among the Huguenots who were urged to revolt against the increasing religious persecution. But though many Huguenots responded, Calvin and responsible ministers were flatly opposed to co-operation. As yet, the Huguenot Church was true to the political theory of Calvinism which taught passive obedience and forbade rebellion. Modern research has definitely exploded the old idea that this Conspiracy was a Protestant revolt. It was political, not religious, its purpose being to replace the Guise by the Bourbons in the government of the country; and most of the armed bands directed to assemble at Amboise consisted of those professional soldiers who were unemployed and in distress. Condé appears to have had plenty of money to hire them; indeed, the financial backing of the Conspiracy so far exceeded anything that the leaders could have raised from their own resources that one French historian has voiced the suspicion that Elizabeth of England was paymaster of the forces.

The plot miscarried; one armed band after another was captured. At first the government was merciful, but as more and more soldiers were seized and the true extent of the Conspiracy became apparent, mercy was replaced by rigour.

But the government was shaken by the evident signs of unrest and discontent, for on top of the Conspiracy came a spate of seditious pamphlets, peddled secretly through the country and even thrown into the royal apartments. These attacks on Guise rule gave Catherine de Medici her excuse to intervene and virtually assume the guiding authority in the State. She sought the advice of Coligny, stopped the operation of the edicts of persecution, released those imprisoned for their religion, and inaugurated a policy of conciliation by which the secular authorities, though ordered to suppress Huguenot assemblies, were forbidden to try any individuals for heresy. They were to leave such trials to the ecclesiastical authorities, which in fact meant that heresy as such would go practically unpunished. So far as the secular law was concerned, the policy amounted to liberty of conscience, but not liberty of worship. In actual practice conciliation went further, for the amnesty to religious offenders and the stopping of the old persecution tended to paralyse the whole secular attack on heresy; an effect which Catherine, in her pursuit of appeasement, was not inclined to prevent. The Huguenot movement took fresh courage; it grew in numbers and in turbulence.

Pacification was a hopeless quest. Though Condé, by putting on a bold face and denying all complicity in the Conspiracy of Amboise, had narrowly escaped punishment, like an inveterate gambler he set to work to build up a new conspiracy. It was on much the same lines as the old, and once more he made his appeal to Protestants, within and without France. This time, significantly enough, the Huguenot movement was more ready to entangle itself. Bands of armed men were raised, and their instructions, as finally evolved, were to join the King of Navarre and Condé as they marched on the Court from Navarre's capital in the south-west. Again the plot miscarried. The Guise got wind of it, secured evidence with which to convict Condé, and then acted vigorously. At Lyons their troops fell on one of Condé's bands which was to have seized the city, after which they set out to crush the Huguenots in that area of France. It looked as if the Religious Wars had already begun.

With equal vigour the government ordered the King of Navarre to bring Condé to Court; and, caught between an army advancing from the north and another that Philip II was assembling in the south, and beguiled by reassuring messages which Catherine de Medici unscrupulously sent him, Anthony obeyed the order and delivered his brother to his fate. Condé was arrested and steps taken to try him for treason; extreme measures for which Francis II may have been personally responsible.

But Fortune had not yet deserted Condé. At this very juncture Francis II was taken ill. In a few days it became evident that he was unlikely to recover, and, with dramatic suddenness, the whole situation was reversed. The new King would be a boy, not yet ten. There could be no pretence this time that the King was of age, nor could the appointment of a Regent be evaded. It looked as if the position for which the Bourbons had twice plotted rebellion was theirs by the constitutional theory of the country. How, indeed, was the claim of Anthony of Navarre, as first prince of the blood, to be denied? And yet that is what Catherine de Medici was determined upon.

She wanted the regency for herself, and with masterly
skill used the last days of Francis II to secure it. By a
mixture of cajolery and coercion, reminding the King
of Navarre of the threatening situation in which their
last plot had placed his family, she persuaded him to
acquiesce in her plan. For his reward she promised the
release of Condé and oblivion as to the past, and the
title of Lieutenant-General of the Kingdom for himself,
a title giving prestige but little or no power.

From the point of view of the country's welfare, it was
thoroughly sound policy. Power was slipping from the
Guise. They were preparing to leave Court, and if
Navarre had become Regent would certainly have
done so, thus placing France once more at the mercy
of the factions, with the roles of Bourbon and Guise
reversed. The Guise were too wealthy and too
mighty for Catherine to let them depart to their
estates, there to brood in pensive discontent. Her aim
was to make friends all round, and with this object in
view she assured Anthony that neither she nor the
Guise had persuaded the dying Francis to arrest his
brother, while Anthony in turn protested his own
innocence. The Guise and he embraced one another.
All was going well and according to Catherine's plan.
On December 5th, 1560, she secured Anthony's renunci-
ation of the regency in writing, and that night the King
died. Charles IX, a boy of nine and a half, was now
King. Catherine placed herself at his side to receive
the homage of the nobility, and placed her bed in his
bedroom to symbolize that dominance over the King from
which he was only to escape once in his unhappy reign.

One more obstacle in the way of Catherine's regency had still to be surmounted. At the time of the

Conspiracy of Amboise it had been decided to summon the Estates General, the national representative assembly. This body had not met for nearly eighty years, and it is eloquent proof of the desperate political and financial condition of the country that the French monarchy, which had hoped to obliterate the memory of such assemblies, was now forced to call them up from the grave.

During the recent troubles, anti-Guise tracts had, among other arguments, declared that the right of appointing Regent and Council during a royal minority belonged to the national assembly; and in Geneva Calvin was at this time supervising an agitation directed to wresting the regency from Catherine de Medici and giving it to the Huguenot King of Navarre. When the Estates General met at Orleans a few days after the death of Francis II, deputations arrived from the Huguenot churches to stimulate the demands of the Estates. But to Calvin's disgust and to the amazement of Bourbon supporters, the King of Navarre refused to play their game, and instead supported Catherine's retention of the regency. The silly man had been completely bamboozled by the Queen-Mother. He was vowing eternal love and friendship for the Guise and complete contentment with everything. The agitation collapsed and Catherine kept the regency.

Appeasement was now the ruling idea, and the year that followed was to see this policy put to its crucial tests. Peace depended on the solution of two problems: Court faction, and religion. Catherine's solution for the first was to keep both Bourbons and Guise at Court, behaving like bosom friends. When their real feelings betrayed themselves in squabbles, she hurried to make them friends again, as one might try to keep two naughty quarrelsome boys in order by love and sweets. It was a nice, motherly policy; but it was not statesmanship, and we shall later see its fatal error.

Catherine's solution for the religious problem, while bound to command respect in the more tolerant atmosphere of later centuries, was no more statesmanlike in its own *milieu* than her handling of the political problem. She contemplated a temporary policy leading to a permanent solution. Temporarily, she determined to continue that partial toleration of Huguenots which had been inaugurated on her initiative during the troubles at Amboise. With this in view she issued a new amnesty, releasing religious prisoners, even those imprisoned for causing disturbances; and at the same time she urged officials to exercise a toleration beyond the terms of her edict. The practical consequence, of course, was to encourage the growth of the Huguenot movement, increase the bitterness of religious feeling everywhere, and make the religious problem graver than ever. The Easter of 1561 was a time of great disorder throughout the land.

It would be a signal error to imagine that Catherine meant either to recognize the Huguenot faith or permanently to tolerate two faiths. Both Calvinists and Catholics would have regarded the latter as sacrilege, and to politicians of that epoch it would have been an assault on national unity. Toleration, as that age saw it, was not homage to the rights of conscience, but the recognition that one of two faiths was not strong enough to suppress the other, or that it would only succeed in doing so at the cost of wrecking the State.

If, then, toleration was merely a temporary policy, what was Catherine's permanent solution for the religious problem? It was a National Council of the French Church with a programme of reform, doctrinal and disciplinary, that would unite Catholic and Protestant.

For some years sovereigns had been urging the Papacy to summon a Council of the whole Church. Such a Council had sat twice at Trent, the last time in 1551-52, when it had adjourned to another meeting. Now this Council had come to decisions that made a compromise between Catholicism and Protestantism, desired by an influential section of Christendom, impossible. Consequently, in demanding another Council those who still hoped for compromise were emphatic that the Council of Trent must be allowed to lapse and an entirely new one be summoned, not bound by its decisions. The Papacy gave no signs of action; and Catherine de Medici and the Cardinal of Lorraine, who in this matter was for compromise with Protestantism and a broad Church settlement, hit upon the plan of calling a National Council of the Gallican Church. They hoped to arrange a compromise with Protestantism, and thus be ready with a *fait accompli* when the Oecumenical Council of the whole Church was at length summoned. The condition of the French Church, they argued, could not wait on Papal dilatoriness.

From the Papal point of view the policy was not only wholly unacceptable but also extremely dangerous. It might lead to schism; and the notorious independence of the Gallican Church made a breach between France and Rome seem far from impossible. The Papacy met the danger by issuing a Bull announcing the continuation of the old Council of Trent, at the same time using all the vigour and threats of which it was capable to prevent the meeting of a French Council.

What was to be done? Catherine could not hold a National Council when an Oecumenical Council was summoned. On the other hand, to acquiesce in the re-summoning of the Council of Trent was to renounce all hope of settling the religious problem in France. She resolved the dilemma by dropping the name of Council from her assembly, disguising her intentions under the term 'Colloquy'; and she proceeded with her plans in secret to avoid a direct Papal veto. Her Colloquy — the Colloquy of Poissy as it was called — was launched on an assembly of the French Church which met at the end of July 1561.

Catherine was playing with fire: there can be no doubt about it. And the Cardinal of Lorraine, who is credited by his latest biographer with responsibility for the scheme of a National Council, revealed, one may admit, a well-meaning tolerance but hardly great foresight or astute statesmanship. In order to arrange the representation of the Huguenot Church at the Colloquy, Catherine naturally turned to the Admiral Coligny, whose charm of manner and unselfish loyalty to the monarchy pleased her. She kept him at Court for advice, agreed to his suggestion that Calvin's right-hand man, Theodore Beza, should be brought from Geneva for the Colloquy, and herself suggested Peter Martyr of Zurich. She actually received these notorious heretics at Court; and inevitably the Huguenots in Court circles, with such leaders present and in high favour, flaunted their faith and worship as never before. Nor could or did all this happen without encouraging the Huguenot movement everywhere.

Catherine's policy could only be justified if it had an appreciable chance of success. In fact it had none. Neither the Catholic Church nor the Calvinist was purely national. Each was controlled from a headquarters over which the French King had no control; and force or cajolery was incapable of imposing a settlement on Rome or Geneva. The truth is that Catherine was blind to the difficulties that she was up against. Her Colloquy would necessarily handle doctrinal problems; but, as a contemporary said, she herself had no idea what the word 'dogma' meant.

The assembly opened. Catherine succeeded in her trick of turning it into a Colloquy. And then the trouble started. Orthodox Catholics cried out in horror at a figure of speech used by Beza. She smoothed this out. Then, when further difficulties arose, she tried to overcome them by gathering the leading Catholic and Protestant divines together in private. She was under the illusion that differences over the Eucharist could be solved as she had been solving the quarrels of Bourbon and Guise in the last nine months — by bringing the quarrelsome people together and persuading them to be friendly. She meant well; she laboured hard; she failed. Fundamental differences of principle are not to be resolved by mediators who have no principles.

Catherine's policy was a catastrophe. On the one hand, by seeming to give recognition to their faith she had bred in Huguenot ranks a new spirit of daring that displayed itself in the wholesale seizing of churches. On the other hand, she had enraged the Catholics, who turned on the Huguenots and massacred them. But in spite of all this, Catherine persisted in her policy of seeking for a peaceful settlement. She kept Beza and Coligny at Court to pacify the Huguenots and check excesses by their influence. What wonder if this merely added to the demoralization, apparently confirming the impression that the Court supported the Huguenots? So thoroughly did she play her game that Beza himself thought that he was about to convert the King and the Queen-Mother to Calvinism!

The extent of the catastrophe has been only half told. In tackling the problem of political faction, Catherine had concentrated all her attention on maintaining friendship between Bourbon and Guise and keeping both parties at Court. Time and again she patched up their quarrels; but all the reconciliations were hollow and of short duration. Meanwhile, in constant pursuit of an elusive goal she had neglected the Montmorency, that vital centre group whose firm loyalty to the Crown made it the essential basis of a King's party. The way was thus free for Guise and the Constable Montmorency, dropping their long and traditional rivalry, to draw together. Both were now opposed to the Bourbons; both felt their Catholic faith threatened by the Queen-Mother's policy.

The result of this tragic neglect was seen when in April 1561, the Constable Montmorency, the Duke of Guise, and another nobleman formed what was known as the Triumvirate — a Catholic party or league. It marks a turning point in our story. For now a party existed, menacing in its power, whose object was to defend the Catholic faith, apart from the King and if need be against him.

The Crown was thus isolated between two parties of passion — Catholic and Huguenot — with all the Court factions on one side or the other. It was unable to control events or prevent the outbreak of civil war: indeed, by flirting with heresy and so fanning the flames of religious strife, Catherine de Medici had unwittingly hastened the day when the calamity of civil war would fall on France.

THE MASSACRE OF ST. BARTHOLOMEW

WE have seen how dangerously short-sighted was Catherine de Medici's policy of appeasement. With an optimism as striking as it was foolish she had set out to succeed where the Emperor Charles V had failed — to effect a compromise in religious doctrines between Catholic and Protestant. She handled the Colloquy of Poissy in August and September 1561 like a Court intrigue; and inevitably failed. She merely stimulated the growth and insolence of the Huguenot party, enraged the Catholics by the favour shown to heretics, and thus intensified the religious passions of the country. France emerged from the Colloquy a long step nearer civil war.

At the same time she had made a fatal blunder in the way she tackled the problem of Court faction. Here she had been so busy keeping Guise and Bourbon in artificial friendship that she had entirely neglected the middle party upon which the independence of the monarchy ought to have been based in a crisis — the party of the Constable Montmorency. The consequence of this neglect was that Guise and Montmorency drew together and formed an alliance in defence of Catholicism. The Crown was left to manœuvre without any real strength of its own between two parties of passion.

But manœuvring was the very genius of this well-meaning woman; and in the autumn and winter of

1561-62 she was feverishly busy with it. She pursued her policy of a peaceful settlement with all the obstinacy and assurance of which her remarkable vitality was capable.

There seems little doubt that at this time she was overestimating the strength of the Huguenot party, and thought it irresistible; as, indeed, by her own misguided encouragement she was doing her best to make it. She kept the Genevan leader Beza and the Admiral Coligny at Court, hoping with their cooperation to restrain the excesses of the Huguenots throughout the country and to work out an immediate policy, which, while satisfying the Huguenots by its extended toleration, would yet avoid clashes with the Catholics. That policy was embodied in the famous edict of January 1562; and, such was Catherine's adroitness, she managed to get the edict passed as the advice of a special, enforced Council. It gave official recognition to the Huguenot Church by permitting worship in the suburbs outside towns, and in the country, though assemblies within towns, where they were likely to provoke Catholic attacks, were forbidden. Even Huguenot synods and consistories were allowed to meet, with the permission of the magistrates, a permission they were told to grant.

Catherine's tactical skill at this time was really astounding. Although in October the Papal Nuncio had been writing to the Pope urging him to form a league with Spain and the other Catholic princes to aid the French Catholics against the Queen-Mother and the Huguenots, now in January Catherine actually succeeded in persuading the Papacy to look favourably on her Edict of Toleration as a necessary concession to avoid greater concessions. She even revived doctrinal talks between Catholic theologians at Court and the Calvinists; and — astonishing spectacle — the Papal representative was seen listening to a Protestant sermon and psalm-singing. At the same time, through Beza and Coligny, Catherine persuaded the Huguenots to acquiesce in the restrictions of her Edict.

But behind this façade of success was an alarming and well-nigh desperate situation. The more hot-headed of the Catholic nobility had watched with increasing hostility Catherine's relations with the Huguenot leaders. She had succumbed to the charm both of Beza and Coligny, and turned more and more to the latter for advice. It seemed as if government policy were passing into the control of Coligny and the Protestant party, and so well were things going with the Huguenots at Court that Protestant worship there was quite open and many were either converted to the new faith or toyed with it. When a bishop announced his conversion, the evil effect of Catherine's conduct could no longer be ignored.

To retain the leading Catholics at Court in such a situation was impossible. The Duke of Guise left in October 1561, and there was a general exodus of Catholic nobility that month. They had already been discussing the possibility of taking up arms against the Protestants, and the Nuncio had made his suggestion to the Papacy of a Catholic league. In mid-November all Europe was talking of the possibility of armed intervention by the Catholic powers.

And then came the final blow. For some months the despicable Anthony of Navarre — Julian the Apostate, as the Huguenots were to call him — had been preparing to rat once more. In December he finally went over to the Catholic Triumvirate, who were plotting to use him in the same way that Calvin had intended just a year before; that is to say, they proposed to support his constitutional right to the regency and depose Catherine de Medici. One noble lord exclaimed that that woman ought to be thrown into the Seine.

In face of this menace, Catherine lost her head. Thinking that the Catholics were about to rise and invite an invasion of France by other sovereigns, she turned to the Huguenot nobles and asked them to discover what forces the Huguenot churches could raise in defence of the monarchy. Coligny sent a circular letter to the various provincial synods and through them to the consistories, and soon was able to tell Catherine that two thousand one hundred and fifty churches and more offered their persons and services at their own expense.

Again Catherine had blundered; blundered seriously, for her action encouraged the Huguenots to complete their military organization, with the result that the direction of their policy passed from the more cautious ministers, schooled in the Calvinist doctrine of passive obedience, to the captains and nobles who were their military leaders. Moreover, when war did at last come, her action presented the Huguenots with the invaluable argument that they were really fighting for the King.

Catherine had now placed herself in the position of manœuvring, not between two political and religious parties, but between two hostile armies.

Her difficulties were multiplying. The Edict of January, granting toleration to the Huguenots, had to be registered in the various *parlements* or high courts of justice, and, though she was able to browbeat the provincial *parlements* when they resisted and thus without much difficulty get her way, coercion was not so successful with the *Parlement de Paris*. This body did not capitulate before March, and by then its resistance had stirred up the religious passions of the city. At Court, Anthony of Navarre created trouble by demanding the dismissal of Coligny and his family. Perhaps it would have been wiser if Coligny had defied the King of Navarre and stayed at Court. Instead, he withdrew, leaving the Huguenot cause in the hands of a woman — Catherine — who was notoriously variable, and of the Prince of Condé, who was hot-headed and irresponsible; and Catherine disliked Condé.

In this situation a spark was enough to cause an explosion; and on March 1st, 1562, there occurred the affray known as the Massacre of Vassy. While passing through his territories, the Duke of Guise came across a Huguenot assembly worshipping in the town of Vassy, contrary to the Edict of January. In the course of the squabble that followed his men killed thirty of the congregation and wounded one hundred and twenty or thirty. During the last year or so there had been plenty of massacres on both sides; but coming at this inflammatory moment and being the work of the Duke of Guise, it was the incident that precipitated war. Condé was at Paris, free from the restraining advice of Coligny, and he sent out a call to arms to the Huguenot churches.

Catherine tried to stop the outbreak of hostilities. She ordered the Duke of Guise, who was marching on Paris with a large armed following, to leave his followers and come to Court. Instead, he joined the Constable and the third Triumvir and together they entered Paris with two to three thousand men. Then Catherine wrote to Condé urging him to come to Court and protect her children, herself, and the Kingdom; an invitation which might have prevented war if it had been accepted, but not being accepted, simply lent additional speciousness to the Huguenot claim that they were taking up arms to protect the King. Finally, she appealed to Coligny; but he too failed to rise to the occasion, and so the Triumvirs were able to march on the Court, leaving Catherine no option but to submit with as good grace as possible to the Catholic army. The Catholics were thus able to enter on war with the person and authority of the King on their side; and soon Catherine's enforced submission was transformed into willing co-operation when Condé, with singular lack of decency, or indeed of foresight, published her confidential appeal to him for help.

Both sides rather drifted into war than entered it suddenly. But in fact the country was already in plain revolution. In April a mob at the city of Sens had fallen on a congregation of Huguenots worshipping, as they had the legal right to do, outside the city walls, and slaughtered all but a few hidden by Catholic friends. Afterwards they slew the captain or guard of the congregation and his men, who happened to be away from the city at the time of the massacre. The passions aroused everywhere may be illustrated by the action of the children on this occasion, who tied a rope about the captain's feet and dragged his body through the streets for hours, crying: 'Bring out your swine, here is the swineherd'.

In this first of the Religious Wars both sides appealed for outside help, the Catholics and Catherine asking for aid from Spain and Savoy and the Huguenots from German Protestants and Elizabeth of England. It was a sign of that tendency, present right through this period — a tendency of more than academic interest to us today — for a general European war to break out over conflicting ideologies. Nor is it without interest to notice how far *real politik* and not mere community of creed determined the action of princes, even of Philip II.

At any rate, there can be no illusion about Queen Elizabeth's realism. Her ambassador in France, who to give him his due was a hotgospeller and crusader, put the inducement this way: France was about to be carved up by Spain and Savoy and other powers, and Elizabeth had better be in at the game and get her share. Elizabeth gave her help — restricted help — on terms: the Huguenots were to give her Havre at once, and at the end of the war she would exchange it for Calais. Condé's agreement to these terms was a measure of his folly as well as his desperation: he made himself infamous as a Frenchman.

The war went excellently for Catherine de Medici: it eliminated all her generals! Anthony of Navarre was killed — a marvellous stroke of luck for her, and good riddance from almost every point of view; one of the Triumvirs was killed; the Duke of Guise, another of the Triumvirs, was assassinated; and the third Triumvir, the Constable Montmorency, was captured. On the Huguenot side Condé was captured. One might say that Catherine had had the devil's own luck. All she had to do to end the war was to let the two captives,

Montmorency and Condé, negotiate the terms; and being captives, they were good peacemakers.

From the point of view of the Huguenot ministers, Condé in these peace negotiations sold the pass. The Pacification of Amboise, in March 1563, conceded liberty of conscience, but in the vital matter of liberty of worship it imposed severe restrictions, from which, however, Condé's own class, the high nobility, was exempted. Lesser folk were permitted to hold Protestant worship only in Huguenot towns or in the suburbs of one town in each bailiwick, while in the Paris region there were to be no Huguenot assemblies.

After securing peace between Frenchmen, Catherine turned the united country — with Condé trying sheepishly to excuse his conduct to Elizabeth — on the English, and drove them out of Havre.

But was it peace? In one sense, yes; because four years were to elapse before war broke out again, and that is not a negligible length of time. On the other hand, no prophetic gifts were needed to see trouble ahead.

In the first place, the assassination of the Duke of Guise in the late war was a crime which was ultimately expiated in the Massacre of St. Bartholomew. The assassin was a young Huguenot nobleman, who was captured and, before being torn in pieces by four horses, accused Coligny of having employed him to do the deed. He alternately maintained and retracted his accusation. Coligny published a reply denying the accusation, and there seems no reason to doubt his word; but with rather unfortunate honesty he went on to declare that he was glad Guise was dead, as he was an enemy of God and the King. Neither he nor Beza had a single word of condemnation for the crime; and extreme Huguenots celebrated the death of the tyrant Guise and bemoaned the execution of the martyr-assassin in floods of poetry, hailing the latter as 'the happy man chosen of God', 'the tenth Paladin, the liberator of France'. Is it any wonder that the widow and son of Guise regarded Coligny as his murderer? or that assassination — a crime hitherto despised in France as a pestiferous Italian custom — rapidly found its way into French life?

Moreover, there emerged from the first Religious War the significant fact that the major part of the nation was Catholic. Catholicism had begun to stir itself and pay more attention to its spiritual duties; and on the Huguenot side recourse to arms had been a mistake. 'If it had not been for the war', wrote the Venetian ambassador, 'France would be at present Huguenot, because the people were so rapidly changing their faith and the ministers had acquired such credit among them that they persuaded them whatever they wished. But when they passed from words to arms and commenced to rob, ruin, or kill . . . the people began to say, "What sort of a religion is this?"'

Catherine de Medici had been prone — as the Venetian ambassador had obviously been — to over-estimate, and overestimate seriously, the strength of the Huguenots. The war broke that spell for her; and though she was still intent on her policy of moderation, and, through the death of the Catholic leaders in the late war, was far better placed to make concessions, her new grasp of realities was shown by her determination not to extend the peace settlement of Amboise but rather to apply it strictly. The result was an undercurrent of Huguenot dissatisfaction, for not only did many find it difficult to worship except by travelling some distance, but the restrictions also erected a serious obstacle in the way of their propaganda.

Real peace in France was not achieved. Religious passion and mob violence continued; and the situation in many places can be suggested by the following reminiscence of a Huguenot gentleman: 'I have often heard my mother say that, just before I was born, she several times had the greatest difficulty to save herself from being drowned like others of all ages and sexes by a great lord of the country, a persecutor of religion. He had them thrown into a river close by his house, saying that he would make them drink out of his big saucer.'

In 1564 Catherine began a tour of France to show the King to his people, a tour which lasted till the beginning of 1566 and included the famous meeting with the Spanish Court at Bayonne in June and July 1565. One might easily leave the Bayonne meeting out of Catherine's story if it were not for its legendary importance and its effect on future events. Catherine's main object in going to Bayonne was to meet her favourite daughter Elizabeth, who had been married to Philip II as part of the peace settlement of Cateau-Cambrésis in 1559. She hoped to persuade Philip II himself to be present, and to bring off a double marriage for her children with his family.

The notion that Catherine at this time was harbouring any sinister and far-reaching plan against Protestantism may certainly be dismissed as false. But fiction no less than fact has its role in human affairs; and it is not difficult to understand why this particular misconception took root. Calvinist propaganda had spread from France into the Spanish Netherlands, and was threatening to create as much trouble there as in France. Hence a meeting between the rulers of Spain and France quite naturally gave rise to rumours that a united front was forming against Protestantism; what we to-day should describe as a Madrid-Paris axis. Philip II no doubt would have liked this. But its one-sided character was too obvious: it would merely have saddled the French with the terrible task of trying to suppress their own Huguenots in order to save Spain in the Netherlands. And, in point of fact, the French government would have rejoiced to see Spanish power in the Netherlands break.

Philip II did not go to Bayonne. His place was taken by the Duke of Alva. The problem of heresy was discussed, and there was mention of a league between France, Spain, and the Emperor. But it is certain that no league was made. All the same, the Huguenots suspected the worst, as democratic Europe, with more reason, suspected the worst from a meeting of Hitler and Mussolini in pre-war days. Ardent Protestants throughout western Europe expressed their fears; and the nightmare of a Catholic league against Protestantism, which began to haunt even Englishmen, found its reputed origin in the interview at Bayonne. When the Massacre of St. Bartholomew occurred seven years later, it was immediately said to have been planned at this nefarious, but in fact quite innocuous, interview.

By the year 1567 affairs were again going badly at the French Court; the nobility full of quarrels, and Catherine de Medici once more engendering deep distrust. She was being too clever by half, promising Philip II to suppress the Huguenots, and telling the Huguenot leaders the opposite. To the Huguenots the limitations on freedom of worship remained a constant source of discontent, and when, in this year 1567, the Duke of Alva took a large army from Spain to the Netherlands and began his rule of terror there, French Calvinists followed the fortunes of their Netherland brethren with much the same passionate interest and fear that many of our own contemporaries were displaying a few years ago, when democratic principles were being overthrown on the Continent; wondering when their turn would come. In reality, so far was Catherine from welcoming Alva's plans, that she refused permission for his army to march through France, and watched the growth of his military power in the Netherlands with anxiety. But the Huguenots could not know this. They had no faith in her, and when the news reached them that Alva had treacherously seized two of the Netherland leaders, Egmont and Horn, the French Huguenot leaders feared that Catherine intended to play the same trick on them. It was a desire to get their own blow in first, rather than anything else, which led them to revolt and attempt to seize the King by surprise at Meaux in September 1567.

In this way began the second Religious War; surely an indication that in the circumstances of the time civil war was endemic. The war did not last long. It was over by March 1568, and only one battle was fought in which the old Constable Montmorency — he was seventy-five — was mortally wounded.

But it was a truce rather than a peace. Killings and drownings went on unofficially, and more people are said to have been murdered after the publication of the peace than were killed in the war. Nor is this surprising, for a significant reaction had set in, and everywhere

Catholics were forming themselves into local leagues, pledged and armed to withstand the Huguenots. A definite change had also come over Catherine de Medici. Every instinct — of maternal jealousy and of royalty — had been shocked by the Huguenot attempt to seize the King; and she was now convinced that they were aiming not so much at religious appeasement as at a political revolution. She abandoned her policy of moderation, dismissed the Chancellor with whose name it was associated, and in her new temper did indeed plan to seize the Huguenot leaders, Condé and Coligny, as Alva had seized Egmont and Horn. However, secrets were not easily kept at Court: news of the plan reached its intended victims, and the third Religious War broke out in consequence in August to September 1568.

This was the longest of the wars hitherto, and the most cruel. 'We fought the first war like angels,' said a Huguenot leader, 'the second like men, and the third like devils.' Whether or not 'angels' was the appropriate word for the first war, 'devils' certainly was for the third. They slaughtered women and children, and wreaked particular vengeance on Catholic priests. They took an abbey and compelled the monks to hang each other. They put garrisons to death in spite of the terms of capitulation, and in cases of direct reprisal showed absolutely no mercy. One city, guilty of the merciless sacking of a Huguenot city, was stormed, its soldiers and inhabitants put to the sword, and the city burnt.

On the Catholic side there was equal or greater savagery. At Orleans, where the Provost of the city had interned the Huguenots in the prisons, the Catholic mob was roused by its preachers; some ran to one of the prisons and put everyone there to death, while others went to a second prison and, being unable to break down the door, set fire to it. Many were burnt to death; others, after throwing their children from the walls in the hope of saving them and seeing them caught on pikes or cut to pieces, jumped themselves and were slaughtered in the same way. Two hundred Huguenots were said to have been killed in this outbreak of mob violence. At Auxerre the mob killed a hundred and fifty Huguenots, stripped their bodies, dragged them through the streets and threw them into the river or into the sewers. Catholic soldiers often showed a similar fury. On one occasion, at the storming of a château, they dragged the Marquis from his sick-bed and threw him into an oven, while on other occasions they made captives jump to their death from the highest tower of a castle. Some commanders tried to stop these bestial cruelties, but others, like the Catholic Monluc, who boasted of his deeds in his Memoirs, employed terrorism as a general policy.

In the first important battle of the war Condé was killed: he was shot in the back after being wounded and after the battle was over. If anything, his death was a gain for his side, since the leadership now passed to the Admiral Coligny. With his ambition and his factious inclinations, Condé had been the evil genius of the Huguenot movement, and he more than anybody had been responsible for the supremacy of its military and disorderly elements.

The manner of Condé's death was yet another sign of that moral anarchy which was soon to culminate in the Massacre of St. Bartholomew. And appropriately enough, there were some remarks made by Catherine de Medici at this time which furnish us with a glimpse into the unprincipled mind from which that infamous act was to spring. On one occasion she told the Spanish ambassador that she proposed to offer a free pardon and fifty thousand crowns to anyone who killed Coligny, with smaller rewards for the murder of his brother and another leader; and in fact, a reward for Coligny's murder was officially proclaimed. On a later occasion she told the ambassador that he would soon see 'a service to God and this King so remarkable that Philip II and the world will rejoice over it'. And when peace came, she assured the Papal Nuncio that it was merely a device to lure Coligny and his followers to Court in order to lay hands on them. Seen in retrospect, these statements might appear to have a sinister bearing on the events of Bartholomew's Eve, 1572. But their real and only significance is psychological: they reveal the unscrupulous, Italianate mind of that woman. Her remark to the Nuncio, for example, was probably just any old tale to keep her stocks high in Papal circles.

Peace came at last; the Peace of St. Germain in August 1570. There had been a growing desire for it, shared by both sides and accentuated by the misery of the country and the appalling state of government finance. Moreover, the influence of the Guise party at Court had been waning. The war had naturally brought the Guise back to power, and the Cardinal of Lorraine had come to rule the roost at Court. His overbearing nature and his insolence to Catherine de Medici and others had turned them against him. There was also a general revulsion, which Catherine shared, against Spanish influence at Court. In fact, a new party was arising; a party known as the Politiques — in contrast with the *dévots* or *réligieux* — moderate Catholics, liberal in their tendencies, who thought first of the good of the State and 'preferred the repose of the Kingdom and their own homes to the salvation of their souls; who would rather that the Kingdom remained at peace without God than at war for Him'. The chief nobleman of this party was Francis de Montmorency, the eldest son and heir of the old Constable Montmorency, killed in 1567. His politique outlook enabled the age-long feud of Montmorency and Guise to break out again; and the fall of the Guise party at Court was his opportunity.

Catherine, too, was switching over to a politique outlook — to a policy of holding the balance between the parties. And, as she so often did, she was associating her new policy with matrimonial projects. She proposed to marry her daughter, Margaret, to Henry of Navarre, the young heir of Anthony and titular head of the Huguenot party. This would bring another crown into the family. And she was also planning to marry her second son to Elizabeth of England — yet another prospective crown.

Obviously, these matrimonial projects, involving in each instance union with a Protestant, called for the support both of the Politiques and the Huguenots, and it is therefore not surprising that the Peace of St. Germain brought these two parties into power in place of the Guise. Nor is it surprising that the Huguenots were granted a measure of toleration which went somewhat further than ever before. Under Politique and moderate Huguenot leadership the new policy marched. True, wooing Queen Elizabeth was a discouraging, though hardly dreary business; but in May 1572, Catherine obtained from England — not a wedding, but what seemed a far from unsatisfactory substitute, a defensive alliance against Spain, known as the Treaty of Blois. It needed time to show that Elizabeth's diplomatic *finesse* could outmatch even that of Catherine.

But though the situation might seem promising, it was not free from danger. The Politiques believed, as did Coligny, that the way to ensure internal peace was to follow a policy of religious toleration at home and sink domestic differences in a national war against the country's great rival, Spain. There was a sound instinct in this, for though the treaty of Cateau-Cambrésis in 1559 had put an end to Franco-Spanish hostility over Italy, geographical facts inexorably drove the two countries to enmity. Spain and its outlying territories held France like a nut in a pair of nutcrackers, with the Spanish Netherlands in the north, Luxemburg and Franche-Comté in the east, then northern Italy, and finally a salient — Roussillon — into south-western France. It was vital to French interests to break this encirclement, but equally vital to Spain to maintain it, for the artery of the Spanish Empire in Europe — the line of communications between Spain and her invaluable Netherland possessions — ran through the territories to the east of France.

The revolt of the Netherlands offered France the chance of weakening her rival and possibly of securing lands in a natural area for French territorial expansion. And when in April 1572 a new and hopeful phase of the Revolt started with the capture of Brille by the Sea-Beggars, the time for seizing that chance seemed to have arrived. So, at least, thought the Politiques;

and so, of course, did the Huguenots, especially the Admiral Coligny. What is more, the King, Charles IX, shared their enthusiasm.

This last is the significant fact; the fact from which begins the story of St. Bartholomew. Something extraordinary had happened: for the first — and the last — time in his life Charles IX had thrown off his mother's tutelage. Coligny had come to Court, captured the affection of the young King, and drawn him enthusiastically into his war plans, even to the point of allowing an army of Huguenots to march secretly against the Spaniards. And this had been done without Catherine's approval or knowledge.

As the Queen-Mother saw the situation, it was perilous in the extreme. Coligny had stolen her son from her: the crime of crimes in her jealous eyes. He was also leading France to her destruction, for his policy meant war with Spain — a war which France would have to fight alone. Catherine was quite right in believing that no support could be expected from England. In fact, English interests and Elizabeth's policy were firmly opposed to France encroaching on the Netherlands seaboard: Elizabeth infinitely preferred to see the Spaniards there, and in the event of war she would at best have maintained an unfriendly neutrality. Not less disturbing to Catherine was the realization that a war policy could only have the effect of confirming Coligny's influence over the King.

These thoughts pointed to one conclusion — the elimination of Coligny; and neither her own unprincipled mind, which had already, in the late war, contemplated such a deed, nor the increasing lawlessness of the times, was likely to cause Catherine any qualms about murdering the Huguenot leader. Her instrument and her opportunity were both at hand. Her instrument was Henry, Duke of Guise, whose father, the late Duke Francis, had been murdered in the first Religious War. The Guise family, as we have seen, firmly believed that Coligny had employed the assassin to do that deed. Nothing could shake their belief nor placate their desire for vengeance; blood called for blood. The new Duke had demanded from the King the right to exact reparation by a duel, but had been refused. Assassination remained the only way.

Catherine's opportunity was the marriage of her daughter Margaret to Henry of Navarre, which took place on August 18th, 1572, and along with the rest of the great nobles, brought practically the whole Huguenot high nobility to Paris to honour their leader's marriage. Catherine was a fool to choose a highly explosive occasion like this, when the nobility of both factions were in town, to exact her revenge on one man; and she ought to have foreseen what would happen. However, choose the occasion she did. There can be very little doubt that she authorized the Guise family to carry out their blood feud and assassinate Coligny.

On August 22nd, as Coligny was returning home from the Court, an arquebus was fired at him from the window of a house, but instead of killing, it merely smashed a finger and wounded him in the arm. With sure instinct the Huguenot nobles at once fixed the blame on the Duke of Guise, angrily demanded justice, and swore that if they did not get it from the King, they would execute it themselves. The King, for his part, was genuinely indignant at the attempt on the Admiral's life, and promised an inquiry into the deed.

Catherine found herself in a dreadful quandary. Responsibility for the assault was bound to be traced to the Duke of Guise, and with equal certainty he would insist on her sharing it. And so, if no worse happened, the devil's game of civil war would start again. In such situations people are thrown back on their deeper promptings, and in her desperation Catherine seized on an idea that was then in the air. Her daughter's marriage, by bringing the leading Huguenot noblemen from all over the country to Court, had presented a unique opportunity of getting rid of them all at a blow; an opportunity which a generation that knew its classical history and recalled the story of Tarquin and the poppies could not fail and had not failed to perceive. It was this idea that Catherine seized upon. In other words, a frantic woman determined to save herself and rescue France from its deadly plague of religious strife, by the wholesale murder of the Huguenot leaders in Paris.

On the night of August 23rd — the day after the attack on Coligny, and St. Bartholomew's Eve — Catherine told her son, the King, of her share in the attack and played on this neurotic boy's feelings until she had persuaded him to consent to a general slaughter of the Huguenots.

In the early morning of August 24th the order was given; the tocsin — the signal for the citizens of Paris to rise — was rung, and the massacre began. The Duke of Guise had charge of the murder of Coligny and of the Huguenot leaders, lists of whom were prepared so that not a single person should escape; while the King himself gave the order which drove the Huguenot gentlemen in the royal palace of the Louvre into the arms of the assassins. Lesser folk were left to be slaughtered by the citizens. Our nerves to-day, when similar passions have inflicted on the world so many and such appalling bestialities, are perhaps too numb to register all the horror that many generations have felt at the scenes of the Bartholomew Massacre. But it was a dreadful, inhuman affair. Neither age nor sex was spared, and many a brute seized the chance to murder an old enemy, whether Huguenot or not. The slaughter went on for several days. One or two of the Huguenot leaders had the good fortune to get away, though every effort was made to catch and kill them. Apart from the two young princes of the blood, Henry of Navarre and the Prince of Condé, not a single Huguenot leader was to have been allowed to escape.

From Paris the news spread to the provinces and royal orders were verbally given to kill the Huguenot leaders there. True, these orders were cancelled by later instructions; true, also, it scarcely needed orders to provoke massacres in those provinces — rather less than half in number — where they occurred. Nor of course was the slaughter confined to the leaders of the Huguenots.

Estimates vary as to the number of victims. Probably three to four thousand were killed in Paris, and as many more in the provinces. One Parisian, a butcher by trade, boasted that he himself had killed four hundred on Bartholomew Day.

The news of the Massacre was received in other countries in varying moods, according to the religious sympathies of rulers and people. Philip II wrote to

Catherine that the punishment 'given to the Admiral and his sect was indeed of such value and prudence and of such service, glory, and honour to God and universal benefit to all Christendom that to hear of it was for me the best and most cheerful news which at present could come to me'. The Venetian Senate voted its congratulations; the Duke of Tuscany acted similarly. At Rome the Pope assembled all the cardinals, told them the news, and went with them to chant a *Te Deum*. He had a medal struck in honour of the event and frescoes painted at the Vatican. And in her communications with Catholic rulers, Catherine took full credit for a clever and meritorious, not to say holy deed.

But in the Protestant world there was horror and indignation; and Catherine was by no means inclined to cut herself adrift from the alliance with England or her useful relations with the German princes and Swiss cantons. She therefore invented one tale after another in her search for an explanation of the Massacre that Protestant rulers, for diplomacy's sake, could swallow.

In both Catholic and Protestant circles, in France as well as abroad, there were many people who believed that the Massacre was a long-premeditated plan. Many Protestants were convinced that it had originated at the famous interview at Bayonne in 1565. The question has been one of the favourite controversies of history; and although historians have long been almost unanimous in rejecting the idea of premeditation, they still feel that it is a problem which must be discussed in any book on the period. It would not be difficult to do as Lord Acton did in a well-known essay written in 1869, and marshall evidence for the older verdict that seems very weighty. And on finding the Papal Nuncio, after the event, writing that Catherine thought 'no one ought now to doubt that these things had happened in accordance with a long-thought-out plan of which she had spoken to me before at Blois', one's first instinct might very well be to convict her out of her own mouth. But the truth is that this woman, an adept at diplomatic prevarication, was weaving such a web of conflicting lies round the Massacre that it behoves us to avoid falling into the trap of believing anything that she said. Most scholars to-day are agreed that in a desperate situation she seized on a desperate plan — a plan which had been talked of by many people beforehand, and must have been there, ready to assert itself in her mind. Had Coligny been killed instead of being merely wounded, in all likelihood there would have been no Massacre of St. Bartholomew. Equally, if the Massacre had really been premeditated, it is extremely unlikely that the efficient execution of the plan would have been jeopardized by a preliminary and isolated attempt on Coligny's life.

It remains to add that there is no evidence to suggest that Catherine ever felt any remorse for her deed.

THE CLOSE OF THE RELIGIOUS WARS

CATHERINE DE MEDICI hoped that the Massacre of St. Bartholomew meant the final destruction of the Huguenots as a militant party. Coligny was dead; and indeed his loss was irreparable. Nobody in the future bridged the two elements of the Huguenot movement — the nobility and the churches — as he had done. Most of the other leaders were also dead. The two titular heads of the party, the young princes of the blood, Henry of Navarre and Henry, Prince of Condé, were virtually prisoners at Court; and, terrified by the Massacre, they announced their conversion to Catholicism. When Catherine saw them at their first Mass she laughed in triumph.

Appearances seemed to justify her, for in addition to the loss to the movement by slaughter, a large number of Huguenots, especially among substantial bourgeois, recanted in terror. But though the Bartholomew Massacre stripped the Huguenot movement of its fringe of members who lacked the stomach to face adversity, and robbed it, for the time being, of its leaders among the high nobility, the ministers were ready to assume leadership, and the common people, especially in Huguenot cities like La Rochelle, remained faithful. In the new period leadership by the high nobility was to be more or less absent until, as we shall see, the Politiques linked up with the Huguenots; and even then ministers and people were more prominent than in pre-Bartholomew years.

Thus Catherine's policy of annihilation was a failure. She laughed too soon. When the King sent a governor to take over control of La Rochelle in September 1572, the ministers and people refused to admit him, and the King was obliged to dispatch an army to capture the city. Its resistance was heroic, and at last in July 1573 the government was forced to admit failure and make a peace granting to La Rochelle, and to other towns which had also revolted, liberty both of conscience and worship. Huguenots elsewhere were granted liberty of conscience only.

The restarting of civil war was not the only effect of the Massacre of St. Bartholomew. In the sphere of political theory Huguenot apologists had hitherto been careful to maintain their loyalty to the King, and to square their actions with the theory of the divine right of kings, to which school of political thought Calvin belonged. Loath to claim any right of resistance, they had been careful to argue that they were in fact fighting for the King, to free him from the control of the Guise Party. Their argument may seem to us a mere pretext; but the change which took place in their attitude after August 1572 shows it was more than that. In the Massacre of St. Bartholomew the Crown had perpetrated an impious act, for which there could be no forgiveness; and Huguenot writers now deliberately attacked the monarchy, making use of the distinction between a king and a tyrant and plundering the Old Testament and classical history for examples of tyrannicide and liberators. Brutus appeared in their text alongside Judith, and Tarquin of course was there as an example of a tyrant. They were concerned with expounding the rights of subjects against tyrants — *vindiciae contra tyrannos*, to quote the title of their most famous post-Bartholomew tract.

Nor did the Huguenots stop at theory. Their movement, as we have seen, was strong in the south of France, in the Midi and Languedoc. Here, as in La Rochelle, they rose in revolt after Bartholomew, and found strong support among the nobility. They ignored the peace of July 1573, remained in arms, and proceeded to frame a rebel government. Languedoc was divided into two governments, centred at Nîmes and Montauban, each with a Count at the head controlled by an elected council or estates, which in important matters consulted the estates of each diocese. The two supreme councils were given control of finance, and money was obtained by levying taxes on towns and villages, whether they were Huguenot or Catholic. During subsequent years this organization and its powers were extended. Here indeed was a state within a state, a separate republic which had virtually displaced the King and sent representatives to him, demanding the free exercise of religion throughout the realm and other sweeping concessions, which the King dared not grant and yet dared not refuse outright.

Still another grave danger threatened the government as the result of the Massacre. It came from the Politique party, whose anger had been aroused only in less degree than that of the Huguenots. The Massacre had involved the eclipse of their policy and their annihilation as a party of power, while many of their number, as enemies of the Guise, had narrowly escaped slaughter, and though escaping themselves, had seen their relatives killed. Coligny, for example, was cousin to the dead Constable Montmorency's several sons: his murder added to the vendetta between the two factions. After Bartholomew the Politiques were a party longing for vengeance on the Guise and for the overthrow of that intolerable woman, Catherine de Medici, along with her foreign favourites. In other words, Court faction was once more linking itself with religious discontent. The old and sordid tragedy was to be played anew.

The Politiques wanted a leader, a new Condé. They could not get Henry of Navarre or the young Condé, since both were virtually prisoners at Court. They therefore aimed at securing Catherine's third surviving son, the Duke of Alençon, that engaging young reprobate whose dashing courtship of Queen Elizabeth provides one of the best comedies of her reign. Alençon was a restless, ambitious young man, jealous of his elder brother, and a great friend of the murdered Coligny. He was quite willing to play the game of the Politiques, provided they could smuggle him away from Court; and during the years 1573 and 1574 there were constant plots for his escape.

Retribution for the appalling crime of St. Bartholomew was obviously approaching; and if this present age had been congenial to the reflection, we might be drawing the comforting conclusion that there are liberties with the moral order which cannot be taken without dire consequences.

On May 30th, 1574, Charles IX died, the second of Catherine's sons to die prematurely. He was barely twenty-four, a nervous and weak youth. Huguenot writers told gruesome stories of the terrors that haunted him in his last days: they point a moral and adorn a tale — no more. At the time of his death his brother and successor, Henry III, was away in Poland playing at being king in that bankrupt and anarchic kingdom; for Catherine de Medici, with her foolish desire to set a crown on all her children's heads, had secured his election to the Polish throne in 1573 and had sent him off, much against his will, into a distant and uncongenial exile. Strange to say, it was because she loved him so much. And that love — he was her favourite son — was now engaging her, with all her accustomed vigour, in securing his French kingdom for him.

A month before Charles IX's death, when his health was clearly giving way, a fresh plot to get Alençon from Court had given Catherine the excuse to strike at the Politiques. She clapped their two leaders — one of them Francis de Montmorency, now head of that House — in the Bastille and made Alençon a prisoner, thus ensuring that no one could prevent her from holding the regency of the kingdom until Henry III got back from Poland, and that no attempt would be made to place Alençon on his brother's throne.

It was smart policy — as St. Bartholomew had been; and retribution followed the one as the other. In fact, Catherine had got her son, Henry III, into a paralysing situation by her action. When she arrested Montmorency she thought that his younger brother, Damville, governor of Languedoc, who was far and away the ablest of the Montmorency-Politique group, had fallen into a net set to catch him. Had he done so, she would doubtless have executed her Bastille prisoners. But Damville was too clever. He escaped the net and saved his brother's life by the surest method — by uniting with the Huguenot organization of Languedoc and erecting an independent republic that Catherine simply dared not defy.

Thus Catherine's subtlety had merely driven the most powerful Politique into the Huguenot ranks. All France south of the Loire was in due course proclaimed to be under Damville as governor and general chief, while he in turn acknowledged the supremacy of the Prince of Condé, who had escaped from Court and was safe in Germany. A veritable republican government was elaborated, with a Council of State to advise Damville, an Assembly of Deputies, Provincial Councils, offices of Justice and Finance, four Law Courts, and a financial division of the whole area. Customs duties and taxes were levied, and this revolutionary organization ran its own police, schools, and hospitals. Condé and Damville were assigned specified salaries, and money and authority were provided to levy troops abroad.

France seemed to be breaking in two. And to make matters worse, the royal Treasury was empty. Charles IX's funeral had cost a great deal of money, still more had been sent to the new King to pay the expenses of his journey back to France; and when Catherine tried to raise loans at Venice and Florence, she failed. Still more significant, she could not raise a loan at Lyons, even at fifteen per cent interest, for three of the chief financial houses of that city had gone bankrupt, and Lyons, like Antwerp, the chief financial capital of Europe, was saying farewell to its departing financial greatness. Catherine had no money to pay her troops, and in the next year the Crown was to make a partial default in its dividends on the *rentes*, the first ripple of that state bankruptcy which came in 1580.

There was little or no hope of Henry III being able to face Damville and his combination of southern moderate Catholics and Huguenots. And when in September 1575 Alençon at last succeeded in escaping from Court and joined the revolt, to be followed in February 1576 by Henry of Navarre, capitulation was the sole option left to the Crown. Capitulation is the only suitable description for the Peace of Monsieur which Henry III made in May 1576. Official regrets were expressed for the Massacre of St. Bartholomew, and concessions were made to the Huguenots amounting to practically complete religious liberty, with devices to ensure their being carried out. The terrorism of St. Bartholomew was thus written down as a failure.

But permanent appeasement had not yet arrived. It was indeed unattainable without a strong monarchy to enforce it; and the monarchy under Henry III was disastrously weak, not only financially but also in the character of the King. Henry III was a case for the Freudian psychologist. He was subject to bursts of energy, and then would let everything go hang. Here is a contemporary's description of him when he arrived at Lyons to face the appalling political problems that I have just described. 'The King goes every night to balls and does nothing but dance. During four whole days he was dressed in mulberry satin with stockings, doublet, and cloak of the same colour. The cloak was very much slashed in the body and had all its folds set with buttons and adorned with ribbons, white and scarlet and mulberry, and he wore bracelets of coral on his arm.' He had spells of gay and dissolute life, and then would join bands of flagellants, wandering about the streets, disguised and with their faces covered and sometimes in bare feet, chanting psalms and scourging each other. When he was in these religious moods, or when he felt disinclined for business, nothing would induce him to attend to affairs of state; at other times he would brook no interference with his authority, not even from his mother. He was the one child of Catherine de Medici who, so far from being dependent on her, actually made her fear him. She continued to play a leading part in the government of the country, as active as ever in the bewildering turns of policy, and apparently almost as powerful; but from now on it was a regime of intermittent dyarchy.

Henry soon began to gather round him a set of young courtiers who were contemptuously called mignons; men who dressed and behaved like dandies, wearing their hair long, 'crimped and recrimped in the most artificial way', their heads sitting on their ruffs 'like the head of John the Baptist on a platter'. They spent their time gambling, swearing, fighting, and dancing; and their conduct gave rise to unspeakable satires. 'Princes of Sodom' was how a satirist described the members of a new order of chivalry founded by the King. It was madness; but there was a dash of state-craft in it. For these mignons were the sons of lesser nobility, owing their whole fortune to the King; men from whom Henry might fashion a new aristocracy by heaping wealth, honour, and high office on them. They were reliable courtiers, fearing and honouring their master 'more than God'; and they were courageous and daring.

Some years later the King developed a passion for lap-poodles, lavished huge sums of money on them and took scores of them wherever he travelled, with a whole retinue of attendants to look after them. How could the monarchy be strong or respected in such a person? The House of Valois was certainly heaping contempt on itself before dying out. And yet it would be unfair to think only of the ridiculous side of Henry III. As one sees him in the dispatches of the English ambassador, he often appears as the able man he was, and as a clever and liberal-minded statesman. But this was not the impression that he made on French noblemen; and the psychological twist in his personality was fatal for the prospects of France.

A King who was always shocking the Court with his pranks, who, in the midst of financial chaos, lavished money on his pleasures and questionable amusements and was incapable of sustained effort in anything, would have been unable, even if he had wished, to reconcile the Guise party and ardent Catholics to the drastic concessions made to heretics by the Peace of Monsieur. As a matter of fact, Henry himself felt the humiliation of the Peace and was determined to find a way of release from the oath binding him to observe it. Action, however, was taken out of his hands, for Catholics in various parts of the country, under the leadership of Henry, Duke of Guise, and with encouragement from Spain, began to band themselves together into a Catholic League.

Here was the old situation of the time of the Triumvirate being re-created — two organized and armed parties of passion, with the monarchy, helpless, between. Henry III met the danger by placing himself at the head of the League and sending orders to the governors of the provinces to recruit members for it, thus forming an army against heresy, but an army under the King, not Guise, and at very little cost to the Crown. The future was to show how dangerous a Catholic League could be when separate from the Crown, and therefore how clever Henry III's manœuvre was. But of course he could only carry it out at the cost of renewed war with the Huguenots. Fortunately for Henry, the Huguenots in this war lacked the assistance of either Alençon or Damville. They were defeated, and in September 1577 were forced to accept a much more limited freedom of worship.

At this point, I think the historian who tries to maintain any significance and simplicity in his narrative and carry the interest of his readers with him, must surrender to the confusion of the whole story and jump, with only a hint or two of what was happening, to the year 1584, when the welter of petty, anarchic, and unedifying detail suddenly shapes itself into a clear pattern.

In the interval between 1577 and 1584 the country became more and more unsettled, despite the unflagging endeavours of Catherine de Medici, who spent sixteen months in an exhausting perambulation of the provinces, coping with universal discontent; at Court the mignons continued to provoke hatred and strife; there was ever-deepening financial gloom, accompanied by increased taxation and suffering almost beyond endurance among peasants and gentry; and of course there was another religious war — if indeed so grave a name should be given to a revolt which was brief, involved only a fraction of the Huguenot party under Henry of Navarre, and seemed so obscure in its origins that legend has given it the frivolous title of The

Lovers' War. The Duke of Alençon, during these years, turned his restless ambition into two external adventures: intervention in the Netherlands on behalf of the rebels there, and his final, breath-taking courtship of Queen Elizabeth. In both enterprises — even that of the Netherlands, which might well have plunged France into the final calamity of war with Spain — he secured support from the King, for the relations between these two remaining sons of Catherine de Medici had long been so bitter, and their quarrels, for all their mother could do, so constant and even scandalous, that Henry III was thankful, at any price, to be rid of a domestic nuisance and danger. He both hated and feared his brother.

In June 1584 fever put an end to Alençon's adventures and started the last phase of Henry III's troubles. Alençon's death had a dramatic effect on the whole situation in France, for it left the country with a prospect that no keen Catholic could face with equanimity — the prospect of a heretic king. Henry III was the last of the Valois. It was obvious that he would die childless. And the heir to the throne was the leader of the Huguenot party, Henry of Navarre.

The Guise family and the Catholic leaders acted rapidly. In September 1584 — Alençon had died in June — they banded themselves together, and some three months later made a treaty with Spain constituting a Holy League, an offensive and defensive alliance for the extirpation of heresy in France and the Netherlands; and in place of Henry of Navarre they recognized his aged and colourless uncle, the Cardinal Bourbon, as successor to the French throne. The League spread rapidly. In Paris a similar organization had come into being independently. At first secret, its founders had divided up the city into sections, each with a leader, and adherents were gained one by one. Then, preachers were set to work to play on the passions of the people; pamphlets were written; and Paris was in process of being whipped up by Catholic demagogues to play the role that its mob played in the Revolution of 1789.

Once more the Crown found itself isolated between the parties. Henry III and Catherine tried to persuade Henry of Navarre to turn Catholic. In all likelihood, he already foresaw that conversion would one day be inevitable, but he refused to take the step now. Wisely; for he would have surrendered the support of his party and placed himself without resources in the hands of the Guise party and the untrustworthy Henry III.

The League did not wait on events. With Spanish money it set about raising armed forces, including foreign mercenaries, and then confronted the King with the necessity of making his choice of sides. Catherine de Medici, intent as usual on appeasement, set off to see the Duke of Guise and try to prevent war. She was old, suffering torments from gout and a multitude of other ailments, and had frequently to negotiate from her bed. The effort was magnificent, but fruitless; Guise negotiated with an army behind him and an ultimatum as his argument. The King had no alternative but to surrender; and at the dictation of the League he was forced in July 1585 to issue an edict revoking all past edicts of pacification, banning heresy, exiling all Protestant ministers, and giving their adherents the alternative of conversion to Catholicism or exile. Henry of Navarre declared that one half of his moustache turned white when he was told of the edict.

I have said that the King had no alternative. He did indeed have the heroic one of refusing to put the stamp of royal authority on a body that was allied to Spain — the national enemy of France — and was precipitating a war in which Spain would have the excuse to intervene. Had Catherine been more nationally minded or Henry III more courageous, anything might have seemed better than surrender. Henry's position was in truth desperate; and no better proof could be cited than the state of his financial credit. In the autumn of 1586 merchants were demanding fifty per cent interest for loans to him.

The edict proscribing Protestantism led to war — the war known as the War of the Three Henries; Henry III, Henry Duke of Guise, and Henry of Navarre. During its course Henry of Navarre gave an indication of the fine military qualities he possessed by winning a brilliant victory in a pitched battle. But the war dragged on. More and more it became evident that the King was an unwilling partner and that he and his mother were doing their rather futile best to bring about peace, while more and more Guise and his adherents showed their contempt for the person and authority of the King and their determination to pursue their own ends in defiance of him.

The League devised a new oath for its members, binding them to obey the King only so long as he proved himself a Catholic and did not favour the heretics. And on the invitation of the Paris leaguers, city after city linked itself by contract with the capital. The situation at Paris was rapidly deteriorating into rebellion against the King. Priests, acting as demagogues, were inflaming passions and attacking the orthodoxy, morality, and policy of the King, while Madame de Montpensier, sister of the Duke of Guise, a redoubtable and fearless woman who harboured a mortal hatred of Henry III and swayed the mob with her fanaticism, was there to urge on and direct the pulpit propaganda. It accomplished more, she declared, than her brothers' armies. The execution of Mary Queen of Scots in England in February 1587 was a heaven-sent opportunity to this vixen; and it was at her suggestion that one of the Paris priests posted in a cemetery a huge picture, showing, in a series of harrowing scenes, all the agonies and tortures to the final bloody spectacle of the traitor's death, through which Catholics were made to pass in Protestant England. The moral for France — that this was the fate awaiting Catholics if the Huguenot Henry of Navarre succeeded to the throne — was obvious, and was brought home to the crowds of excitable Parisians who flocked to the cemetery.

For rather more than a fortnight Henry III dared not do anything. Then he had the poster taken down at night, and two months later arrested three of the leading priestly agitators. Parisians sounded the tocsin and rose in revolt. The trouble died down; but the League had discovered its strength. France was passing into confusion, from which a wavering King was unable to save it.

The critical moment in this final struggle of authority against insolence could not be far off. It came in the famous Day of Barricades at Paris in May 1588. The League had urged the Duke of Guise to come to Paris: the King ordered him not to enter the city. He arrived on the 9th of May with nine companions only; and soon a crowd of thirty thousand was following him in triumphal procession through the streets. Making his way to Catherine de Medici's lodging, and then, with her, to the Louvre, he bowed to the King, explained that he had disobeyed the royal command and come to Paris to justify himself, and finally withdrew unmolested to his own house. Pope Sixtus V, whose wise and penetrating remarks on the ability of Queen Elizabeth and the naval strength of England have an arresting frankness, made the apt comment on this occasion: 'Guise', he said, 'was a reckless fool to put himself in the hands of a King whom he was insulting; the King was a coward to let him go untouched.'

Guise had defied his sovereign; and Henry III had now to choose whether he would resume his authority by overthrowing the citizens, or surrender, or flee from his own capital. He tried the first: the people of Paris, organized and equipped by their leaders, threw up barricades, isolated the King's forces in small bands, and having surrounded them, compelled them to lay down their arms. Then, while his mother pretended to negotiate with Guise, Henry slipped out of Paris and escaped. Guise was left 'King of Paris'.

Henry III had fled from Paris; but not to fight. He had left his mother temporizing with the Duke of Guise, and negotiations went on while the Duke replaced loyal officials in Paris with out-and-out Leaguers, sent to stir up the Leaguers in other cities, writing of the King with disdainful insolence, and — to put it briefly — built up an impregnable position for himself. The terms which the King was forced to concede in the Edict of Union in July 1588 were those of complete surrender. He placed almost absolute authority in the hands of the Duke of Guise, and in foreign as well as domestic policy granted practically everything that the League demanded. Guise was received at Court and made Lieutenant-General of France.

Humiliations continued to descend on the wretched King. The Duke of Savoy, a petty princeling, thinking that France was disintegrating, had the impudence to invade a part of French territory and seize it. Then when the Estates General met at Blois in October, instead of finding that assembly loyal, Henry discovered that the League had 'made' the elections and that still further humiliations were to be inflicted upon him.

But the end of the King's patience had been reached. The defeat of the Spanish Armada by the English in July-August had freed him from any fear of Spanish intervention, and in September he had summarily dismissed those of his ministers who were the creatures of his mother, thus breaking from Catherine de Medici's control and from her policy of appeasement. He turned to those noblemen whose interests were likely to suffer most from Guise ambition. A feeling of approaching catastrophe was in the air. A Tuscan diplomat had written home to say that 'the day of the dagger will come'; and on all sides the Duke of Guise was being warned of a plot against his life, and urged, but in vain, to leave the Court.

Henry and his little circle of new advisers discussed the possibility of trying the Duke for treason. But he was too powerful for legal action to be taken against him. The dagger was the only way. On December 23rd at 7.30 in the morning Guise came to a Council meeting at the Château of Blois, to which the King had summoned him. When he and his brother, the Cardinal of Guise, had arrived, mounting the famous outside staircase that led to the Council Chamber, the doors were closed behind them and a solid body of guards filled the staircase. The meeting began; the King, waiting in a cabinet off the adjoining royal bed-chamber, sent for the Duke. As he approached, the door through which he came was locked, the King's bodyguard of gentlemen formed up behind him and then fell on him and murdered him. The Cardinal of Guise was seized, imprisoned, and the next day, as he in turn went to answer the royal summons, was struck down and murdered. Others were imprisoned, including the leaders of the League in the Estates General; but bloodshed stopped with the slaughter of the two chiefs.

The King had carried out this drastic coup without consulting his mother. Afterwards, he broke the news to her. She was lying ill in bed, and less than three weeks later died, bemoaning — so it was said and may be believed — the fate that she saw would befall the last and best beloved of her sons.

Like Catherine de Medici when she perpetrated the Massacre of St. Bartholomew, Henry III believed that his bloody purge would put an end to the troubles of France; that the League would collapse. He failed, as Catherine had failed, to appreciate that behind political ambition and intrigue there was genuine and deep religious feeling and popular fanaticism. At Paris the priests preached revolt and the citizens responded, while the Sorbonne, following the example of Huguenot writers after August 1572, placed its moral and intel-lectual authority on the doctrine that it was lawful to take up arms against tyrants. Children marched through the streets of Paris, led by their curés and others, all carrying torches, which from time to time they dashed to the ground, crying 'So may God quench the race of Valois'.

It was war, not peace that the King gave to France. The League took the field, while Henry III allied himself with the King of Navarre and the Huguenots. The war went in favour of the two Kings. They laid siege to Paris, and it seemed as if the city, for all its fanatical ardour, was lost, when the inevitable happened. In the mood created by the murder of the Guise, even the blackest of all crimes, regicide, took on the semblance of a noble action. On August 1st, 1589, a young Dominican friar, Jacques Clément, whose fanatical purpose seems to have been aided by Madame de Montpensier and others, made his way into Henry III's presence and mortally wounded him with a knife. Thus perished the last of the Valois kings. He was thirty-eight years of age. When the people of Paris heard the news, they placed tables in the streets, drank, feasted, sang, and danced.

Henry III had survived his mother by only seven months. The Age of Catherine de Medici was ended.

Though the future course of the Religious Wars lies outside the scope of our subject, we must briefly round off the story. The new King, Henry of Navarre—Henry IV, as he now was — had to begin the reconquest of the country all over again. Some of the royalist nobility who had followed Henry III placed their loyalty to France before too ardent a pursuit of religious aims, and were content with the prospect that the new King would in due time turn Catholic; but others withdrew, so that the army sank to half its numbers and Henry IV had to retire on Normandy and begin his campaign from there.

It was a long, long task. But though fortunes waxed and waned and years passed by, the ultimate odds were all in Henry IV's favour. In the first place, France at last had got what it needed most, a strong man as King. Henry IV had his shortcomings, but they were essentially Gallican; part of a personality that the French loved. On the manly side, his courage, his ability to face hardship, his capacity for leadership, and his *bonhomie*, all were qualities that he possessed in a remarkable degree. He was a great and a charming man. And one fact is certain: had France possessed such a King in 1559, or even later, its history would have been startlingly different.

As for the League, in the long run its strength was its weakness. Paris, under the leadership of fanatical demagogues, played a supremely heroic and dramatic part in the resistance to Henry IV. But the fanaticism of its leaders led to excesses, suggestive of the Terror during the French Revolution, which alienated moderate people, stimulated the growth of a politique section of the League, and at last so wore out the nerves of the citizens that reaction set in. The ardour of their welcome to peace and a legitimate King, when they arrived, surprised everyone.

The foreign support which the League received, while time and again its salvation, proved an embarrassment in the end, and aided Henry IV. The League had no obvious rival to proclaim King when the fainéant Cardinal of Bourbon died, a captive, in May 1590. The King of Spain aimed at securing the throne for his daughter; the Duke of Savoy — another foreign ally of the League — coveted the throne, or, at any rate, a section of south-east France; and members of the House of Lorraine harboured conflicting aspirations. It was a monstrous situation, against which the national sentiment of France was ultimately bound to revolt.

At long last, in July 1593, the time was ripe for the proper solution of the problem, one that Henry IV had foreseen for years: he allowed himself to be converted to Catholicism. And in March 1594 he reaped his reward by entering Paris amid the plaudits of the people. He was quite cynical in his readiness to buy off the self-seeking, recalcitrant Catholic leaders still arrayed against him; and gradually the troubles dwindled into a war against Spain only. Even this ended in May 1598.

A month before — in April — Henry had finally liquidated the religious problem of France by the Edict of Nantes. It established toleration — liberty of conscience and liberty of worship — on a liberal but not quite complete scale, and granted full civil rights to the Huguenots, instituting special law courts to secure them justice. It also conceded certain political guarantees which left the Huguenots something of a state within a state, thus recognizing that the Edict was not merely a concession to a section of the community, but a treaty between two warring powers. Such was the cleavage in the French nation effected by thirty-five years of intermittent strife. In the next century Richelieu abolished the political guarantees in the name of national unity, and Louis XIV, in the name of religious unity, revoked the edict of toleration. France returned to One King, One Faith, and that Faith, inevitably, the Catholic Faith.

*   *   *

As we look back on this dismal story of the French

Religious Wars, what are our reflections? What, in particular, are we to think of Catherine de Medici, on whom, if there was any personal responsibility for events, that responsibility must in the main rest? How far was her policy at fault? How far were the qualities and defects of her character involved? How far was she the victim of uncontrollable circumstances? Should we, perhaps, echo the indulgent verdict of Henry IV, who said, 'What more could one poor woman, with a handful of children, do?'

Undoubtedly, the root of the trouble was the weakness of the monarchy. It was a calamity for France that the crisis of its religious problem coincided with the successive accession to the throne of two children and a period of thirty years of incompetent kingship. Even if there had been no Queen-Mother, with a lust to rule, and if the premier prince of the blood had been an able man, it is doubtful whether he could have saved the country from civil war.

Quite irrespective of her ability, Catherine de Medici was deplorably handicapped. Her sex, her birth, her foreign origin were all chinks in the armour of her prestige. John Knox had blown the Blast of sixteenth-century mankind against the Monstrous Regiment of Women. 'I am assured', he wrote, 'that God hath revealed to some in this our age that it is more than a monster in nature that a woman should reign and bear empire above man.' Women, he declared, were painted forth by nature to be weak, frail, impatient, feeble, and foolish; they were the port and gate of the Devil; their covetousness, like the gulf of Hell, was insatiable. For the weak to nourish the strong, the foolish to govern the discreet, in brief, for women to rule men, was contumely to God and the subversion of good order and justice. The Bible, the Fathers, Aristotle, and the Classical world were at one on the subject; and men, he thought, were less than the beasts to permit such an inversion of God's order. Knox blew his blast against the regency of a Queen-Mother, Mary of Guise, in Scotland, and the rule of a woman, Mary Tudor, as Queen of England. The stridency of his trumpet may have been peculiar to himself, but the tune it played was acceptable to most men of his day. As a noble author of Henry VIII's reign wrote: 'Indeed, God did not create this kind — women — unto rule and to have governance, and therefore they never reign prosperously.' It was a fundamental assumption, incalculable in its effects. A foreign ambassador summed up Catherine de Medici's difficulties in the following sentence: 'It is sufficient to say that she is a woman, a foreigner, and a Florentine to boot, born of a simple house, altogether beneath the dignity of the Kingdom of France.' There were few of the many attacks on Catherine which did not drive home one or other, or all, of these points.

The second half of the sixteenth century was prolific in women-rulers: Mary Tudor, Mary of Guise, Elizabeth, Mary Queen of Scots, Margaret of Parma, and Catherine de Medici herself. With one exception — Queen Elizabeth — they must ultimately be written off as failures. But the fact that there is one exception makes us ask how far qualities of character combined with sex to spell success or failure.

Both Catherine de Medici and Elizabeth were essentially feminine in their opportunism, their tendency to see things in a personal rather than an

THE AGE OF CATHERINE DE MEDICI

impersonal way, and — dare one add? or would it be wiser to attribute this to the Renaissance? — their unscrupulousness. But, having noted these similarities of character, we are immediately struck by very strong contrasts. It may be put this way: we can, without too gross a caricature, keep within the characteristics of opportunism, personal bias, and unscrupulousness in describing Catherine. It is impossible to be bound by them in describing Elizabeth.

Elizabeth was a woman of much finer sensibility; she was essentially merciful. It would be quite incongruous to think of her planning a Massacre of St. Bartholomew, and the dagger as a political expedient — save when she grasped at the suggestion, as an alternative to the public execution of Mary Queen of Scots in 1587 — was alien to her. Perhaps it would be unfair to cite her successful assertion of authority, since she was a queen-regnant and Catherine was not. But a question of character also enters here. Elizabeth was a true daughter of Henry VIII; she was to the manner born, and had the reserve of character to carry off her regal supremacy, in spite of her sex: contrast, as French contemporaries did, her handling of the Essex rebellion with Henry III's handling of its French precedent, the Day of Barricades.

Moreover, Elizabeth had a trained intellect. Behind her bewildering opportunism there was a firm grasp of principle. She was a statesman, and Burghley in his old age paid tribute to her greatness as such. Catherine may have been, indeed she was, a woman of practical intelligence, but hers was not a trained mind; she never understood that abstract ideas could even exist, nor that there are occasions when compromise and conciliation are politically as well as morally ruinous. She was completely lacking in the qualities of a statesman.

But the contrast which perhaps mattered most of all — the fundamental distinction between the two women — is that Elizabeth loved her country with the consuming passion that few but women can experience. In her England was personified. Catherine de Medici did not know what patriotism meant. She was always a foreigner; she had no country. Her passion was her children, not France; she was the mother, not the Queen.

I think it needs little reflection to realize that one of the most significant facts in Elizabethan history is England's escape from religious wars; and we may be helped in our final appraisal of Catherine de Medici if we ask how far this immunity was due to better fortune or better policy. Better fortune there certainly was. I have already mentioned one advantage, namely, that Elizabeth was a queen-regnant. But this alone, without the necessary qualities of character to assert her authority and counteract the grave disadvantages of sex, would not have saved England from civil strife. Mary Queen of Scots would probably have failed in Elizabeth's place, and so too would a woman with Catherine de Medici's foreign outlook — this was Mary Tudor's tragedy — her lack of principle, and her matrimonial inclinations. Catherine, in Elizabeth's place, would have married a great prince; therefore a foreigner and a Catholic. And then the fat would certainly have been in the fire.

Again, England had inestimably better fortune in the lack of any princes of the blood, and in the relative weakness of feudal ties and propensities among the nobility. But it is also true that France — at any rate before 1584 — was not exposed to the appalling danger of having a rival claimant to the throne, present for nearly twenty years in the country and posing, as did Mary Queen of Scots, as the leader of the opposite faith. The Northern Rebellion in 1569 might well have been the first of the English religious wars.

England was also fortunate in its insular isolation, which constituted against Catholic missionaries a sanitary cordon that France lacked against Geneva and the German Protestant cities; but of course there is — or perhaps we should say, there was — no really effective cordon against the spread of ideas, and given a weak monarch and mistaken policy England would have drifted into religious wars just as certainly as France.

Perhaps France could not have escaped her fate: with child-kings, for which accident and not Catherine de Medici was responsible, the probability of trouble may have been equivalent to practical certainty. All the same, we have in the course of this narrative noted blunder after blunder in Catherine's policy, and these, coupled with her shortcomings of character and intellect, undoubtedly affected the nature and duration of France's thirty-odd years of disaster.

A final, if brief, comment must be made on the economic effects of the wars. At the beginning of the sixteenth century France was developing its commerce and industry with great rapidity: England in comparison was a backwater. But it was in Elizabethan and Jacobean England that the first industrial revolution — to use a phrase now being applied to this period by economic historians — forged ahead. No doubt there are other reasons than the incidence or absence of war to explain this profoundly important contrast in the economic fortunes of the two countries. In England, unlike France, the legal and constitutional framework of society favoured individualism; there were no *rentes* through which the Crown, under the guise of investment, could divert the savings of the people from economic enterprise into the prodigal ways of royal expenditure; and parliament exercised a control over taxation to which there was no parallel in France. But if the political structure of a society affects its economic structure, the reverse is also true, and it is best to centre one's attention on the two fundamental and interrelated factors in English economic development: the possession by individuals of capital to invest in commercial and industrial projects, and the existence of orderly, peaceful conditions to foster their growth. In France, the financial drain of the Italian Wars had already by 1559 partially exhausted the wealth of the country. The long period of civil strife which followed, with its chronic and continuous state of disorder, its human and material losses, and its costliness, was fatal to economic enterprise: even river and road communications fell into disrepair.

Modern large-scale industry, as the examples of England and the Netherlands demonstrated, could only develop freely at the expense of the old medieval gild system, with its rigid and obstructive control of craftsmen. But sixteenth-century France, instead of witnessing the decay of the craft gilds, saw something approaching a universal extension of this form of constraint, under the authority of the State; and the period of religious wars, with the reconstruction that followed under Henry IV — reconstruction inspired and planned, as was inevitable, by the Crown — clamped State regimentation on the industrial life of France until the eighteenth century. Such large-scale industry as developed was organized, controlled, and in part financed by the Crown, and, instead of being concentrated on the heavy industries and labour-saving devices as in England, was mainly confined to luxury trades and the fine arts, such as silks and tapestries. In England individual initiative broke down gild regulations, waged successful war on the Crown's proclamations and letters patent, and even drove blithely through obstructive statutes. If, like England, France had enjoyed peace and orderly government in the sixteenth century, if wealth had been allowed to accumulate in the hands of individuals, and if a sufficient financial margin had remained with poorer folk to create a market for large-scale industry in goods other than luxuries, who can doubt that individual enterprise would have broken through restraint in that country also, though with less rapidity because the obstacles were tougher? And then, instead of *étatisme* in the political sphere stifling individualism in the economic, we might have seen the opposite process at work in sixteenth- and seventeenth-century France. That, after all, is what happened in the eighteenth century.

Rural life in France suffered terribly from the Wars of Religion. The professional soldiers of the time, whether foreign or native, generally lived on the country and were a curse to friend and foe, pillaging and ravaging almost as a matter of course. Intervals of peace were too often that in name only; disorder bred brigandage, and even the Crown, in its desperate need for money, preyed on the wretched peasants and helped to complete their ruin. 'The length and scale of the war has so desolated the provinces of our Kingdom', wrote Henry IV in 1595, 'that most of the land is deserted and uncultivated.' But if the fate of agriculture was the most spectacular economic disaster of all, it was the least enduring. Fields remain even when they are deserted, and a new generation soon comes along to replace the lost one.

> My father lived at Blenheim then,
> Yon little stream hard by;
> They burnt his dwelling to the ground,
> And he was forced to fly:
> So with his wife and child he fled,
> Nor had he where to rest his head.
>
> With fire and sword the country round
> Was wasted far and wide,
> And many a childing mother then
> And newborn baby died.

It was the same poignant story in sixteenth-century France; but you will remember that Old Kaspar was soon at work again on his father's lands and telling his grandchild Wilhelmine of man's fatuous ways.

BIBLIOGRAPHICAL NOTE

THE following select list of books is intended as a guide to further reading on the subject. Those who desire a fuller list should consult the sectional bibliographical notes in Henri Hauser's authoritative volume, *La Prépondérance Espagnole* (*1559-1660*), in the series *Peuples et Civilisations*, edited by L. Halphen and P. Sagnac (Paris: Alcan. 1933).

ARMSTRONG, EDWARD. *The French Wars of Religion. Their political aspects.* (London: Percival. 1892)

CHOISY, EUGÈNE. *L'État chrétien Calviniste à Genève au temps de Théodore de Bèze.* (Geneva: Eggimann, n.d.)

EHRENBERG, RICHARD. *Capital and Finance in the Age of the Renaissance.* (London: Cape. 1928)

EVENETT, H. OUTRAM. *The Cardinal of Lorraine and the Council of Trent.* (Cambridge: University Press. 1930)

KINGDON, ROBERT M. *Geneva and the Coming of the Wars of Religion in France, 1555-1563.* (Geneva: Librairie E. Droz. 1956)

MARIÉJOL, JEAN H. *Histoire de France*, ed. Ernest Lavisse. Tome VI, i. *La Réforme et la Ligue* (*1559-1598*). (Paris: Hachette. 1904)

MARIÉJOL, JEAN H. *Catherine de Médicis.* (Paris: Hachette. 1920)

NEF, JOHN U. *Industry and Government in France and England, 1540-1640.* (Philadelphia: The American Philosophical Society. 1940)

ROMIER, LUCIEN. *La Conjuration d'Amboise.* (Paris: Perrin. 1923)

ROMIER, LUCIEN. *Catholiques et Huguenots à la Cour de Charles IX.* (Paris: Perrin. 1924)

ROMIER, LUCIEN. *Le Royaume de Catherine de Médicis. La France à la veille des Guerres de Religion.* 2 vols. (Paris: Perrin. 1925)

THOMPSON, JAMES WESTFALL. *The Wars of Religion in France, 1559-1576.* (Chicago: University Press. 1909)

TOUR, P. IMBART DE LA. *Les Origines de la Réforme.* Tome IV. *Calvin et l'Institution Chrétienne.* (Paris: Firmin-Didot. 1935)

VAN DYKE, PAUL. *Catherine de Médicis.* 2 vols. (London: Murray. 1923)

WHITEHEAD, A. W. *Gaspard de Coligny, Admiral of France.* (London: Methuen. 1904)

WILKINSON, MAURICE. *A History of the League or Sainte Union, 1576-1595.* (Glasgow: Jackson, Wylie. 1929)

INDEX

Alençon, Francis of Valois, Duke of, 85, 86, 87, 91, 92
Alva, Duke of, 69, 70, 71

Beza, Theodore, 55, 56, 57, 60, 61, 66
Bourbon, Cardinal of, 92, 100
Bourbon, House of, 42-44, 48, 50, 51, 52, 53, 56, 57, 59

Calvin, John, 16 f., 18 f., 45, 52, 62, 83; against Conspiracy of Amboise, 48
Calvinism, 16ff.
Catherine de Medici, 9 passim; attempt to assassinate Coligny, 77-78; causes St. Bartholomew's Massacre, 78; character of, 41-42, 102-106; matrimonial projects of, 74-75; received heretics at court, 57, 58, 59 ff.; retention of the regency, 50-51, 52; solution for the religious problem, 53-58
Catholic League, 90-91
Charles V, Emperor, 9, 10, 59
Charles IX, 51, 57, 68, 70, 76, 77-78, 79, 83, 84, 85-86, 87
Clement VII, Pope, 40
Coligny, Gaspard de, Admiral, 44, 46, 49, 55, 57, 60, 61, 62, 63, 64, 66, 71, 72, 73, 75, 76, 77, 78, 80, 81, 82, 85; attempt at assassination of, 77
Colloquy of Poissy, 55, 56, 59, 60
Concordat of 1516, 11, 15, 27
Condé, Henry, Prince of, 79, 82, 85, 87
Condé, Louis, Prince of, 42, 46-47, 48, 49, 50, 51, 63, 64, 65, 66, 71; converted to Huguenot faith, 45; death of, 72
Conspiracy of Amboise, 38, 47-49, 52
Council of Trent, 54, 55
credit inflation, first great, 33-34

Damville, Marshal, Governor of Languedoc, 86-87, 88, 91
Day of the Barricades, 95-96, 104
Diane de Poitiers, 40-41

economic effects of the Wars of Religion, 106-109
Edict of January, 60-1, 62-3
Edict of Nantes, 101
Edict of Union, 96
Edward VI (England), 39
Elizabeth, Queen of Spain (daughter of Catherine de Medici), 68
Elizabeth I (England), 9, 14, 18, 35, 48, 65, 66, 74, 75, 76, 85, 92, 96, 103; compared with Catherine de Medici, 104-105
Estates General, 52, 97, 98

First Huguenot National Synod at Paris, 30 f.
Francis I, 27, 33, 40, 41, 43
Francis II, 39, 43, 46, 50, 51, 52
French Calvinists, see Huguenot
French Reform Movement, 11 ff.

Geneva, 22 ff.
German Reformation, 10, 16
Guise, Charles of, Cardinal of Lorraine, 12, 43, 46, 54, 55, 73
Guise, Francis, Duke of, 43, 44, 46, 57, 61, 63, 64, 65, 67, 77; assassination of, 66
Guise, Henry, Duke of, 77, 78, 90, 91, 94, 97; assassination of, 97-98, 99; defiance of Henry III, 95-96
Guise, Louis, Cardinal of, 98
Guise, Mary of, Queen Regent of Scotland, 43, 103
Guise, House of, 42-43, 44, 45, 46 ff., 56, 57, 59, 73, 74, 77, 84, 85, 90, 92, 93

INDEX

Henry II, 9, 11, 34, 35, 37, 39, 40, 43, 44, 46

Henry III, 86, 87, 88 ff., 104; murder of, 99

Henry IV, *see* Navarre, Henry of

Henry VIII (England), 15, 33, 40, 103, 104

Holy League, 92-93, 94, 95, 96, 97, 98, 99, 100

Huguenot movement, 17, 20, 24 ff., 36

Huguenot refugees, 23

Italian Wars, 9, 10, 38, 44, 46; effect on France, 33 ff.

Knox, John, opinion of women, 102-103

La Renaudie, 47

Lutheranism, 13-14

machinery of government (French), 36 ff.

Margaret (daughter of Catherine de Medici), 74, 77

Martyr, Peter, 55

Mary, Queen of Scots, 43, 46, 95, 103, 104, 105, 106

Mary Tudor, 9, 23, 103, 105

Massacre of St. Bartholomew, 23, 42, 66 ff., 81 ff., 98, 104

Massacre of Vassy, 63

Montmorency, Anne de, Constable of France, 43-44, 45, 57, 59, 64, 65, 66, 70, 85

Montmorency, Francis de, 74, 86

Montmorency, House of, 45-44, 45, 57

Montpensier, Catherine de, 95, 99

Navarre, Anthony, King of, 42, 45, 46, 47, 50, 51, 52, 61-62

Navarre, Henry, King of (afterwards Henry IV), 74, 77, 79, 82, 85, 87, 92, 93, 94, 95, 99, 100, 102, 108, 109; conversion to Catholicism of, 101

nobility, plight of the lesser, 37 ff.

non-residence, in the French clergy, 12-13

Pacification of Amboise, 66, 67

Peace of Augsburg, 10

Peace of Cateau-Cambrésis, 9, 11, 33, 39, 68, 75

Peace of Monsier, 88, 90

Peace of St. Germain, 73, 74

Philip II (Spain), 9, 35, 42, 50, 65, 68, 69, 73, 79

pluralism of benefices, 12-13

Politiques, party of, 73-74, 75, 82, 84, 85, 86, 87

Savoy, Duke of, 97, 100

Sixtus V, Pope, 96

Synods, 18, 19 ff.

Thirty Years War, 10

Triumvirate, 62, 64, 65; formation of, 57

War of the Three Henries, 94

74 75   12 11 10 9

harper ⚜ torchbooks

American Studies: General

HENRY ADAMS Degradation of the Democratic Dogma. ‡ *Introduction by Charles Hirschfeld.* TB/1450

LOUIS D. BRANDEIS: Other People's Money, *and How the Bankers Use It. Ed. with Intro, by Richard M. Abrams* TB/3081

HENRY STEELE COMMAGER, Ed.: The Struggle for Racial Equality TB/1300

CARL N. DEGLER: Out of Our Past: *The Forces that Shaped Modern America* CN/2

CARL N. DEGLER, Ed.: Pivotal Interpretations of American History
Vol. I TB/1240; Vol. II TB/1241

A. S. EISENSTADT, Ed.: The Craft of American History: *Selected Essays*
Vol. I TB/1255; Vol. II TB/1256

LAWRENCE H. FUCHS, Ed.: American Ethnic Politics TB/1368

MARCUS LEE HANSEN: The Atlantic Migration: 1607-1860. *Edited by Arthur M. Schlesinger. Introduction by Oscar Handlin* TB/1052

MARCUS LEE HANSEN: The Immigrant in American History. *Edited with a Foreword by Arthur M. Schlesinger* TB/1120

ROBERT L. HEILBRONER: The Limits of American Capitalism TB/1305

JOHN HIGHAM, Ed.: The Reconstruction of American History TB/1068

ROBERT H. JACKSON: The Supreme Court in the American System of Government TB/1106

JOHN F. KENNEDY: A Nation of Immigrants. *Illus. Revised and Enlarged. Introduction by Robert F. Kennedy* TB/1118

LEONARD W. LEVY, Ed.: American Constitutional Law: *Historical Essays* TB/1285

LEONARD W. LEVY, Ed.: Judicial Review and the Supreme Court TB/1296

LEONARD W. LEVY: The Law of the Commonwealth and Chief Justice Shaw: *The Evolution of American Law, 1830-1860* TB/1309

GORDON K. LEWIS: Puerto Rico: *Freedom and Power in the Caribbean. Abridged edition* TB/1371

HENRY F. MAY: Protestant Churches and Industrial America TB/1334

RICHARD B. MORRIS: Fair Trial: *Fourteen Who Stood Accused, from Anne Hutchinson to Alger Hiss* TB/1335

GUNNAR MYRDAL: An American Dilemma: *The Negro Problem and Modern Democracy. Introduction by the Author.*
Vol. I TB/1443; Vol. II TB/1444

GILBERT OSOFSKY, Ed.: The Burden of Race: *A Documentary History of Negro-White Relations in America* TB/1405

CONYERS READ, Ed.: The Constitution Reconsidered. *Revised Edition. Preface by Richard B. Morris* TB/1384

ARNOLD ROSE: The Negro in America: *The Condensed Version of Gunnar Myrdal's An American Dilemma. Second Edition* TB/3048

JOHN E. SMITH: Themes in American Philosophy: *Purpose, Experience and Community* TB/1466

WILLIAM R. TAYLOR: Cavalier and Yankee: *The Old South and American National Character* TB/1474

American Studies: Colonial

BERNARD BAILYN: The New England Merchants in the Seventeenth Century TB/1149

ROBERT E. BROWN: Middle-Class Democracy and Revolution in Massachusetts, 1691–1780. *New Introduction by Author* TB/1413

JOSEPH CHARLES: The Origins of the American Party System TB/1049

HENRY STEELE COMMAGER & ELMO GIORDANETTI, Eds.: Was America a Mistake? *An Eighteenth Century Controversy* TB/1329

WESLEY FRANK CRAVEN: The Colonies in Transition: 1660-1712† TB/3084

CHARLES GIBSON: Spain in America † TB/3077

CHARLES GIBSON, Ed.: The Spanish Tradition in America + HR/1351

LAWRENCE HENRY GIPSON: The Coming of the Revolution: 1763-1775. † *Illus.* TB/3007

JACK P. GREENE, Ed.: Great Britain and the American Colonies: 1606-1763. + *Introduction by the Author* HR/1477

AUBREY C. LAND, Ed.: Bases of the Plantation Society + HR/1429

JOHN LANKFORD, Ed.: Captain John Smith's America: *Selections from his Writings* ‡ TB/3078

LEONARD W. LEVY: Freedom of Speech and Press in Early American History: *Legacy of Suppression* TB/1109

---

† The New American Nation Series, edited by Henry Steele Commager and Richard B. Morris.
‡ American Perspectives series, edited by Bernard Wishy and William E. Leuchtenburg.
a History of Europe series, edited by J. H. Plumb.
§ The Library of Religion and Culture, edited by Benjamin Nelson.
‖ Researches in the Social, Cultural, and Behavioral Sciences, edited by Benjamin Nelson.
╳ Harper Modern Science Series, edited by James A. Newman.
° Not for sale in Canada.
+ Documentary History of the United States series, edited by Richard B. Morris.
# Documentary History of Western Civilization series, edited by Eugene C. Black and Leonard W. Levy.
Λ The Economic History of the United States series, edited by Henry David et al.
¶ European Perspectives series, edited by Eugene C. Black.
** Contemporary Essays series, edited by Leonard W. Levy.
* The Stratum Series, edited by John Hale.

PERRY MILLER: Errand Into the Wilderness
TB/1139
PERRY MILLER & T. H. JOHNSON, Eds.: The Puritans: *A Sourcebook of Their Writings*
Vol. I TB/1093; Vol. II TB/1094
EDMUND S. MORGAN: The Puritan Family: *Religion and Domestic Relations in Seventeenth Century New England* TB/1227
RICHARD B. MORRIS: Government and Labor in Early America TB/1244
WALLACE NOTESTEIN: The English People on the Eve of Colonization: 1603-1630. † *Illus.*
TB/3006
FRANCIS PARKMAN: The Seven Years War: *A Narrative Taken from* Montcalm and Wolfe, The Conspiracy of Pontiac, *and* A Half-Century of Conflict. *Edited by John H. McCallum* TB/3083
LOUIS B. WRIGHT: The Cultural Life of the American Colonies: 1607-1763. † *Illus.*
TB/3005
YVES F. ZOLTVANY, Ed.: The French Tradition in America + HR/1425

American Studies: The Revolution to 1860

JOHN R. ALDEN: The American Revolution: 1775-1783. † *Illus.* TB/3011
MAX BELOFF, Ed.: The Debate on the American Revolution, 1761-1783: *A Sourcebook*
TB/1225
RAY A. BILLINGTON: The Far Western Frontier: 1830-1860. † *Illus.* TB/3012
STUART BRUCHEY: The Roots of American Economic Growth, 1607-1861: *An Essay in Social Causation. New Introduction by the Author.*
TB/1350
WHITNEY R. CROSS: The Burned-Over District: *The Social and Intellectual History of Enthusiastic Religion in Western New York, 1800-1850* TB/1242
NOBLE E. CUNNINGHAM, JR., Ed.: The Early Republic, 1789-1828 + HR/1394
GEORGE DANGERFIELD: The Awakening of American Nationalism, 1815-1828. † *Illus.*
TB/3061
CLEMENT EATON: The Freedom-of-Thought Struggle in the Old South. *Revised and Enlarged. Illus.* TB/1150
CLEMENT EATON: The Growth of Southern Civilization, 1790-1860. † *Illus.* TB/3040
ROBERT H. FERRELL, Ed.: Foundations of American Diplomacy, 1775-1872 + HR/1393
LOUIS FILLER: The Crusade against Slavery: 1830-1860. † *Illus.* TB/3029
DAVID H. FISCHER: The Revolution of American Conservatism: *The Federalist Party in the Era of Jeffersonian Democracy* TB/1449
WILLIAM W. FREEHLING, Ed.: The Nullification Era: *A Documentary Record* ‡ TB/3079
WILLIM W. FREEHLING: Prelude to Civil War: *The Nullification Controversy in South Carolina, 1816-1836* TB/1359
PAUL W. GATES: The Farmer's Age: *Agriculture, 1815-1860* Δ TB/1398
FELIX GILBERT: The Beginnings of American Foreign Policy: *To the Farewell Address*
TB/1200
ALEXANDER HAMILTON: The Reports of Alexander Hamilton. ‡ *Edited by Jacob E. Cooke*
TB/3060
THOMAS JEFFERSON: Notes on the State of Virginia. ‡ *Edited by Thomas P. Abernethy*
TB/3052
FORREST MCDONALD, Ed.: Confederation and Constitution, 1781-1789 + HR/1396

BERNARD MAYO: Myths and Men: *Patrick Henry, George Washington, Thomas Jefferson*
TB/1108
JOHN C. MILLER: Alexander Hamilton and the Growth of the New Nation TB/3057
JOHN C. MILLER: The Federalist Era: 1789-1801. † *Illus.* TB/3027
RICHARD B. MORRIS, Ed.: Alexander Hamilton and the Founding of the Nation. *New Introduction by the Editor* TB/1448
RICHARD B. MORRIS: The American Revolution Reconsidered TB/1363
CURTIS P. NETTELS: The Emergence of a National Economy, 1775-1815 Δ TB/1438
DOUGLASS C. NORTH & ROBERT PAUL THOMAS, Eds.: *The Growth of the American Economy to 1860* + HR/1352
R. B. NYE: The Cultural Life of the New Nation: 1776-1830. † *Illus.* TB/3026
GILBERT OSOFSKY, Ed.: Puttin' On Ole Massa: *The Slave Narratives of Henry Bibb, William Wells Brown, and Solomon Northup* ‡
TB/1432
JAMES PARTON: The Presidency of Andrew Jackson. *From Volume III of the* Life of Andrew Jackson. *Ed. with Intro. by Robert V. Remini* TB/3080
FRANCIS S. PHILBRICK: The Rise of the West, 1754-1830. † *Illus.* TB/3067
MARSHALL SMELSER: The Democratic Republic, 1801-1815 † TB/1406
TIMOTHY L. SMITH: Revivalism and Social Reform: *American Protestantism on the Eve of the Civil War* TB/1229
JACK M. SOSIN, Ed.: The Opening of the West + HR/1424
GEORGE ROGERS TAYLOR: The Transportation Revolution, 1815-1860 Δ TB/1347
A. F. TYLER: Freedom's Ferment: *Phases of American Social History from the Revolution to the Outbreak of the Civil War. Illus.*
TB/1074
GLYNDON G. VAN DEUSEN: The Jacksonian Era: 1828-1848. † *Illus.* TB/3028
LOUIS B. WRIGHT: Culture on the Moving Frontier TB/1053

American Studies: The Civil War to 1900

W. R. BROCK: An American Crisis: *Congress and Reconstruction, 1865-67* ° TB/1283
T. C. COCHRAN & WILLIAM MILLER: The Age of Enterprise: *A Social History of Industrial America* TB/1054
W. A. DUNNING: Reconstruction, Political and Economic: 1865-1877 TB/1073
HAROLD U. FAULKNER: Politics, Reform and Expansion: 1890-1900. † *Illus.* TB/3020
GEORGE M. FREDRICKSON: The Inner Civil War: *Northern Intellectuals and the Crisis of the Union* TB/1358
JOHN A. GARRATY: The New Commonwealth, 1877-1890 † TB/1410
JOHN A. GARRATY, Ed.: The Transformation of American Society, 1870-1890 + HR/1395
WILLIAM R. HUTCHISON, Ed.: American Protestant Thought: *The Liberal Era* ‡ TB/1385
HELEN HUNT JACKSON: A Century of Dishonor: *The Early Crusade for Indian Reform.* † *Edited by Andrew F. Rolle* TB/3063
ALBERT D. KIRWAN: Revolt of the Rednecks: *Mississippi Politics, 1876-1925* TB/1199
WILLIAM G. MCLOUGHLIN, Ed.: The American Evangelicals, 1800-1900: An Anthology ‡
TB/1382
ARTHUR MANN: Yankee Reforms in the Urban Age: *Social Reform in Boston, 1800-1900*
TB/1247

2

ARNOLD M. PAUL: Conservative Crisis and the Rule of Law: *Attitudes of Bar and Bench, 1887-1895. New Introduction by Author* TB/1415

JAMES S. PIKE: The Prostrate State: *South Carolina under Negro Government. ‡ Intro. by Robert F. Durden* TB/3085

WHITELAW REID: After the War: *A Tour of the Southern States, 1865-1866. ‡ Edited by C. Vann Woodward* TB/3066

FRED A. SHANNON: The Farmer's Last Frontier: *...Agriculture, 1860-1897* TB/1348

VERNON LANE WHARTON: The Negro in Mississippi, 1865-1890 TB/1178

American Studies: The Twentieth Century

RICHARD M. ABRAMS, Ed.: The Issues of the Populist and Progressive Eras, 1892-1912 + HR/1428

RAY STANNARD BAKER: Following the Color Line: *American Negro Citizenship in Progressive Era. ‡ Edited by Dewey W. Grantham, Jr. Illus.* TB/3053

RANDOLPH S. BOURNE: War and the Intellectuals: *Collected Essays, 1915-1919. ‡ Edited by Carl Resek* TB/3043

A. RUSSELL BUCHANAN: The United States and World War II. † *Illus.*
Vol. I TB/3044; Vol. II TB/3045

THOMAS C. COCHRAN: The American Business System: *A Historical Perspective, 1900-1955* TB/1080

FOSTER RHEA DULLES: America's Rise to World Power: 1898-1954. † *Illus.* TB/3021

JEAN-BAPTISTE DUROSELLE: From Wilson to Roosevelt: *Foreign Policy of the United States, 1913-1945. Trans. by Nancy Lyman Roelker* TB/1370

HAROLD U. FAULKNER: The Decline of Laissez Faire, 1897-1917 TB/1397

JOHN D. HICKS: Republican Ascendancy: 1921-1933. † *Illus.* TB/3041

ROBERT HUNTER: Poverty: *Social Conscience in the Progressive Era. ‡ Edited by Peter d'A. Jones* TB/3065

WILLIAM E. LEUCHTENBURG: Franklin D. Roosevelt and the New Deal: 1932-1940. † *Illus.* TB/3025

WILLIAM E. LEUCHTENBURG, Ed.: The New Deal: *A Documentary History +* HR/1354

ARTHUR S. LINK: Woodrow Wilson and the Progressive Era: 1910-1917. † *Illus.* TB/3023

BROADUS MITCHELL: Depression Decade: *From New Era through New Deal, 1929-1941* ∆ TB/1439

GEORGE E. MOWRY: The Era of Theodore Roosevelt and the Birth of Modern America: 1900-1912. † *Illus.* TB/3022

WILLIAM PRESTON, JR.: Aliens and Dissenters: *Federal Suppression of Radicals, 1903-1933* TB/1287

WALTER RAUSCHENBUSCH: Christianity and the Social Crisis. ‡ *Edited by Robert D. Cross* TB/3059

GEORGE SOULE: Prosperity Decade: *From War to Depression, 1917-1929* ∆ TB/1349

GEORGE B. TINDALL, Ed.: A Populist Reader: *Selections from the Works of American Populist Leaders* TB/3069

TWELVE SOUTHERNERS: I'll Take My Stand: *The South and the Agrarian Tradition. Intro. by Louis D. Rubin, Jr.; Biographical Essays by Virginia Rock* TB/1072

Art, Art History, Aesthetics

CREIGHTON GILBERT, Ed.: Renaissance Art ** *Illus.* TB/1465

EMILE MALE: The Gothic Image: *Religious Art in France of the Thirteenth Century.* § 190 illus. TB/344

MILLARD MEISS: Painting in Florence and Siena After the Black Death: *The Arts, Religion and Society in the Mid-Fourteenth Century.* 169 illus. TB/1148

ERWIN PANOFSKY: Renaissance and Renascences in Western Art. *Illus.* TB/1447

ERWIN PANOFSKY: Studies in Iconology: *Humanistic Themes in the Art of the Renaissance. 180 illus.* TB/1077

JEAN SEZNEC: The Survival of the Pagan Gods: *The Mythological Tradition and Its Place in Renaissance Humanism and Art. 108 illus.* TB/2004

OTTO VON SIMSON: The Gothic Cathedral: *Origins of Gothic Architecture and the Medieval Concept of Order. 58 illus.* TB/2018

HEINRICH ZIMMER: Myths and Symbols in Indian Art and Civilization. *70 illus.* TB/2005

Asian Studies

WOLFGANG FRANKE: China and the West: *The Cultural Encounter, 13th to 20th Centuries. Trans. by R. A. Wilson* TB/1326

L. CARRINGTON GOODRICH: A Short History of the Chinese People. *Illus.* TB/3015

DAN N. JACOBS, Ed.: The New Communist Manifesto and Related Documents. *3rd revised edn.* TB/1078

DAN N. JACOBS & HANS H. BAERWALD, Eds.: Chinese Communism: *Selected Documents* TB/3031

BENJAMIN I. SCHWARTZ: Chinese Communism and the Rise of Mao TB/1308

BENJAMIN I. SCHWARTZ: In Search of Wealth and Power: *Yen Fu and the West* TB/1422

Economics & Economic History

C. E. BLACK: The Dynamics of Modernization: *A Study in Comparative History* TB/1321

STUART BRUCHEY: The Roots of American Economic Growth, 1607-1861: *An Essay in Social Causation. New Introduction by the Author.* TB/1350

GILBERT BURCK & EDITORS OF *Fortune:* The Computer Age: *And its Potential for Management* TB/1179

JOHN ELLIOTT CAIRNES: The Slave Power. ‡ *Edited with Introduction by Harold D. Woodman* TB/1433

SHEPARD B. CLOUGH, THOMAS MOODIE & CAROL MOODIE, Eds.: Economic History of Europe: *Twentieth Century #* HR/1388

THOMAS C.COCHRAN: The American Business System: *A Historical Perspective, 1900-1955* TB/1180

ROBERT A. DAHL & CHARLES E. LINDBLOM: Politics, Economics, and Welfare: *Planning and Politico-Economic Systems Resolved into Basic Social Processes* TB/3037

PETER F. DRUCKER: The New Society: *The Anatomy of Industrial Order* TB/1082

HAROLD U. FAULKNER: The Decline of Laissez Faire, 1897-1917 ∆ TB/1397

PAUL W. GATES: The Farmer's Age: *Agriculture, 1815-1860* ∆ TB/1398

WILLIAM GREENLEAF, Ed.: American Economic Development Since 1860 + HR/1353

J. L. & BARBARA HAMMOND: The Rise of Modern Industry. || *Introduction by R. M. Hartwell* TB/1417

ROBERT L. HEILBRONER: The Future as History: *The Historic Currents of Our Time and the Direction in Which They Are Taking America* TB/1386

ROBERT L. HEILBRONER: The Great Ascent: *The Struggle for Economic Development in Our Time* TB/3030

FRANK H. KNIGHT: The Economic Organization TB/1214

DAVID S. LANDES: Bankers and Pashas: *International Finance and Economic Imperialism in Egypt. New Preface by the Author* TB/1412

ROBERT LATOUCHE: The Birth of Western Economy: *Economic Aspects of the Dark Ages* TB/1290

ABBA P. LERNER: Everbody's Business: *A Reexamination of Current Assumptions in Economics and Public Policy* TB/3051

W. ARTHUR LEWIS: Economic Survey, 1919-1939 TB/1446

W. ARTHUR LEWIS: The Principles of Economic Planning. *New Introduction by the Author°* TB/1436

ROBERT GREEN MC CLOSKEY: American Conservatism in the Age of Enterprise TB/1137

PAUL MANTOUX: The Industrial Revolution in the Eighteenth Century: *An Outline of the Beginnings of the Modern Factory System in England°* TB/1079

WILLIAM MILLER, Ed.: Men in Business: *Essays on the Historical Role of the Entrepreneur* TB/1081

GUNNAR MYRDAL: An International Economy. *New Introduction by the Author* TB/1445

HERBERT A. SIMON: The Shape of Automation: *For Men and Management* TB/1245

PERRIN STRYER: The Character of the Executive: *Eleven Studies in Managerial Qualities* TB/1041

RICHARD S. WECKSTEIN, Ed.: Expansion of World Trade and the Growth of National Economies ** TB/1373

Education

JACQUES BARZUN: The House of Intellect TB/1051

RICHARD M. JONES, Ed.: Contemporary Educational Psychology: *Selected Readings *** TB/1292

CLARK KERR: The Uses of the University TB/1264

Historiography and History of Ideas

HERSCHEL BAKER: The Image of Man: *A Study of the Idea of Human Dignity in Classical Antiquity, the Middle Ages, and the Renaissance* TB/1047

J. BRONOWSKI & BRUCE MAZLISH: The Western Intellectual Tradition: *From Leonardo to Hegel* TB/3001

EDMUND BURKE: On Revolution. Ed. by Robert A. Smith TB/1401

WILHELM DILTHEY: Pattern and Meaning in History: *Thoughts on History and Society.° Edited with an Intro. by H. P. Rickman* TB/1075

ALEXANDER GRAY: The Socialist Tradition: *Moses to Lenin °* TB/1375

J. H. HEXTER: More's Utopia: *The Biography of an Idea. Epilogue by the Author* TB/1195

H. STUART HUGHES: History as Art and as Science: *Twin Vistas on the Past* TB/1207

ARTHUR O. LOVEJOY: The Great Chain of Being: *A Study of the History of an Idea* TB/1009

JOSE ORTEGA Y GASSET: The Modern Theme. *Introduction by Jose Ferrater Mora* TB/1038

RICHARD H. POPKIN: The History of Scepticism from Erasmus to Descartes. *Revised Edition* TB/1391

G. J. RENIER: History: *Its Purpose and Method* TB/1209

MASSIMO SALVADORI, Ed.: Modern Socialism # HR/1374

GEORG SIMMEL et al.: Essays on Sociology, Philosophy and Aesthetics. *Edited by Kurt H. Wolff* TB/1234

BRUNO SNELL: The Discovery of the Mind: *The Greek Origins of European Thought* TB/1018

W. WARREN WAGER, ed.: European Intellectual History Since Darwin and Marx TB/1297

W. H. WALSH: Philosophy of History: In Introduction TB/1020

History: General

HANS KOHN: The Age of Nationalism: *The First Era of Global History* TB/1380

BERNARD LEWIS: The Arabs in History TB/1029

BERNARD LEWIS: The Middle East and the West ° TB/1274

History: Ancient

A. ANDREWS: The Greek Tyrants TB/1103

ERNST LUDWIG EHRLICH: A Concise History of Israel: *From the Earliest Times to the Destruction of the Temple in A.D. 70 °* TB/128

ADOLF ERMAN, Ed.: The Ancient Egyptians: *A Sourcebook of their Writings. New Introduction by William Kelly Simpson* TB/1233

THEODOR H. GASTER: Thespis: *Ritual Myth and Drama in the Ancient Near East* TB/1281

MICHAEL GRANT: Ancient History ° TB/1190

A. H. M. JONES, Ed.: A History of Rome through the Fifgth Century # *Vol. I: The Republic* HR/1364

Vol. II The Empire: HR/1460

SAMUEL NOAH KRAMER: Sumerian Mythology TB/1055

NAPHTALI LEWIS & MEYER REINHOLD, Eds.: Roman Civilization *Vol. I: The Republic* TB/1231

Vol. II: The Empire TB/1232

History: Medieval

MARSHALL W. BALDWIN, Ed.: Christianity Through the 13th Century # HR/1468

MARC BLOCH: Land and Work in Medieval Europe. *Translated by J. E. Anderson* TB/1452

HELEN CAM: England Before Elizabeth TB/1026

NORMAN COHN: The Pursuit of the Millennium: *Revolutionary Messianism in Medieval and Reformation Europe* TB/1037

G. G. COULTON: Medieval Village, Manor, and Monastery HR/1022

HEINRICH FICHTENAU: The Carolingian Empire: *The Age of Charlemagne. Translated with an Introduction by Peter Munz* TB/1142

GALBERT OF BRUGES: The Murder of Charles the Good: *A Contemporary Record of Revolutionary Change in 12th Century Flanders. Translated with an Introduction by James Bruce Ross* TB/1311

F. L. GANSHOF: Feudalism TB/1058

F. L. GANSHOF: The Middle Ages: *A History of International Relations. Translated by Rémy Hall* TB/1411

W. O. HASSALL, Ed.: Medieval England: *As Viewed by Contemporaries* TB/1205

DENYS HAY: The Medieval Centuries ° TB/1192

DAVID HERLIHY, Ed.: Medieval Culture and Society # HR/1340

J. M. HUSSEY: The Byzantine World   TB/1057
ROBERT LATOUCHE: The Birth of Western Economy: *Economic Aspects of the Dark Ages* °   TB/1290
HENRY CHARLES LEA: The Inquisition of the Middle Ages. || *Introduction by Walter Ullmann*   TB/1456
FERDINARD LOT: The End of the Ancient World and the Beginnings of the Middle Ages. *Introduction by Glanville Downey*   TB/1044
H. R. LOYN: The Norman Conquest   TB/1457
ACHILLE LUCHAIRE: Social France at the time of Philip Augustus. *Intro. by John W. Baldwin*   TB/1314
GUIBERT DE NOGENT: Self and Society in Medieval France: *The Memoirs of Guibert de Nogent*. || *Edited by John F. Benton* TB/1471
MARSILIUS OF PADUA: The Defender of Peace. *The Defensor Pacis. Translated with an Introduction by Alan Gewirth*   TB/1310
CHARLES PETET-DUTAILLIS: The Feudal Monarchy in France and England: *From the Tenth to the Thirteenth Century* °   TB/1165
STEVEN RUNCIMAN: A History of the Crusades Vol. I: *The First Crusade and the Foundation of the Kingdom of Jerusalem. Illus.*   TB/1143

Vol. II: *The Kingdom of Jerusalem and the Frankish East 1100-1187. Illus.*   TB/1243
Vol. III: *The Kingdom of Acre and the Later Crusades. Illus.*   TB/1298
J. M. WALLACE-HADRILL: The Barbarian West: *The Early Middle Ages, A.D. 400-1000*   TB/1061

History: Renaissance & Reformation

JACOB BURCKHARDT: The Civilization of the Renaissance in Italy. *Introduction by Benjamin Nelson and Charles Trinkaus. Illus.* Vol. I TB/40; Vol. II TB/41
JOHN CALVIN & JACOPO SADOLETO: A Reformation Debate. *Edited by John C. Olin*   TB/1239
FEDERICO CHABOD: Machiavelli and the Renaissance   TB/1193
THOMAS CROMWELL: Thomas Cromwell on Church and Commonwealth,: *Selected Letters 1523-1540.* ¶ *Ed. with an Intro. by Arthur J. Slavin*   TB/1462
R. TREVOR DAVIES: The Golden Century of Spain, 1501-1621 °   TB/1194
J. H. ELLIOTT: Europe Divided, 1559-1598 *a* °   TB/1414
G. R. ELTON: Reformation Europe, 1517-1559 ° *a*   TB/1270
DESIDERIUS ERASMUS: Christian Humanism and the Reformation: *Selected Writings. Edited and Translated by John C. Olin*   TB/1166
DESIDERIUS ERASMUS: Erasmus and His Age: *Selected Letters. Edited with an Introduction by Hans J. Hillerbrand. Translated by Marcus A. Haworth*   TB/1461
WALLACE K. FERGUSON et al.: Facets of the Renaissance   TB/1098
WALLACE K. FERGUSON et al.: The Renaissance: *Six Essays. Illus.*   TB/1084
FRANCESCO GUICCIARDINI: History of Florence. *Translated with an Introduction and Notes by Mario Domandi*   TB/1470
WERNER L. GUNDERSHEIMER, Ed.: French Humanism, 1470-1600. * *Illus.*   TB/1473
MARIE BOAS HALL, Ed.: Nature and Nature's Laws: *Documents of the Scientific Revolution* #   HR/1420
HANS J. HILLERBRAND, Ed., The Protestant Reformation #   HR/1342
JOHAN HUIZINGA: Erasmus and the Age of Reformation. *Illus.*   TB/19

JOEL HURSTFIELD: The Elizabethan Nation   TB/1312
JOEL HURSTFIELD, Ed.: The Reformation Crisis   TB/1267
PAUL OSKAR KRISTELLER: Renaissance Thought: *The Classic, Scholastic, and Humanist Strains*   TB/1048
PAUL OSKAR KRISTELLER: Renaissance Thought II: *Papers on Humanism and the Arts*   TB/1163
PAUL O. KRISTELLER & PHILIP P. WIENER, Eds.: Renaissance Essays   TB/1392
DAVID LITTLE: Religion, Order and Law: *A Study in Pre-Revolutionary England.* § *Preface by R. Bellah*   TB/1418
NICCOLO MACHIAVELLI: History of Florence and of the Affairs of Italy: *From the Earliest Times to the Death of Lorenzo the Magnificent. Introduction by Felix Gilbert*   TB/1027
ALFRED VON MARTIN: Sociology of the Renaissance. ° *Introduction by W. K. Ferguson*   TB/1099
GARRETT MATTINGLY et al.: Renaissance Profiles. *Edited by J. H. Plumb*   TB/1162
J. E. NEALE: The Age of Catherine de Medici °   TB/1085
J. H. PARRY: The Establishment of the European Hegemony: 1415-1715: *Trade and Exploration in the Age of the Renaissance*   TB/1045
J. H. PARRY, Ed.: The European Reconnaissance: *Selected Documents* #   HR/1345
BUONACCORSO PITTI & GREGORIO DATI: Two Memoirs of Renaissance Florence: *The Diaries of Buonaccorso Pitti and Gregorio Dati. Edited with Intro. by Gene Brucker. Trans. by Julia Martines*   TB/1333
J. H. PLUMB: The Italian Renaissance: *A Concise Survey of Its History and Culture*   TB/1161
A. F. POLLARD: Henry VIII. *Introduction by A. G. Dickens.* °   TB/1249
RICHARD H. POPKIN: The History of Scepticism from Erasmus to Descartes   TB/139
PAOLO ROSSI: Philosophy, Technology, and the Arts, in the Early Modern Era 1400-1700. || *Edited by Benjamin Nelson. Translated by Salvator Attanasio*   TB/1458
FERDINAND SCHEVILL: The Medici. *Illus.* TB/1010
FERDINAND SCHEVILL: Medieval and Renaissance Florence. *Illus.* Vol. I: *Medieval Florence*   TB/1090
Vol. II: *The Coming of Humanism and the Age of the Medici*   TB/1091
R. H. TAWNEY: The Agrarian Problem in the Sixteenth Century. *Intro. by Lawrence Stone*   TB/1315
H. R. TREVOR-ROPER: The European Witch-craze of the Sixteenth and Seventeenth Centuries and Other Essays °   TB/1416
VESPASIANO: Rennaissance Princes, Popes, and XVth Century: *The Vespasiano Memoirs. Introduction by Myron P. Gilmore. Illus.*   TB/1111

History: Modern European

RENE ALBRECHT-CARRIE, Ed.: The Concert of Europe #   HR/1341
MAX BELOFF: The Age of Absolutism, 1660-1815   TB/1062
OTTO VON BISMARCK: Reflections and Reminiscences. *Ed. with Intro. by Theodore S. Hamerow* ¶   TB/1357
EUGENE C. BLACK, Ed.: British Politics in the Nineteenth Century #   HR/1427

5

EUGENE C. BLACK, Ed.: European Political History, 1815-1870: *Aspects of Liberalism* ¶
TB/1331

ASA BRIGGS: The Making of Modern England, 1783-1867: *The Age of Improvement* °
TB/1203

D. W. BROGAN: The Development of Modern France ° Vol. I: *From the Fall of the Empire to the Dreyfus Affair* TB/1184
Vol. II: *The Shadow of War, World War I, Between the Two Wars* TB/1185

ALAN BULLOCK: Hitler, A Study in Tyranny. ° *Revised Edition. Illus.* TB/1123

EDMUND BURKE: On Revolution. *Ed. by Robert A. Smith* TB/1401

E. R. CARR: International Relations Between the Two World Wars. 1919-1939 ° TB/1279

E. H. CARR: The Twenty Years' Crisis, 1919-1939: *An Introduction to the Study of International Relations* ° TB/1122

GORDON A. CRAIG: From Bismarck to Adenauer: *Aspects of German Statecraft. Revised Edition* TB/1171

LESTER G. CROCKER, Ed.: The Age of Enlightenment # HR/1423

DENIS DIDEROT: The Encyclopedia: *Selections. Edited and Translated with Introduction by Stephen Gendzier* TB/1299

JACQUES DROZ: Europe between Revolutions, 1815-1848. ° *a Trans. by Robert Baldick*
TB/1346

JOHANN GOTTLIEB FICHTE: Addresses to the German Nation. *Ed. with Intro. by George A. Kelly* ¶ TB/1366

FRANKLIN L. FORD: Robe and Sword: *The Re-Louis XIV* TB/1217

ROBERT & ELBORG FORSTER, Eds.: European Society in the Eighteenth Century # HR/1404

C. C. GILLISPIE: Genesis and Geology: *The Decades before Darwin* § TB/51

ALBERT GOODWIN, Ed.: The European Nobility in the Enghteenth Century TB/1313

ALBERT GOODWIN: The French Revolution
TB/1064

ALBERT GUERARD: France in the Classical Age: *The Life and Death of an Ideal* TB/1183

JOHN B. HALSTED, Ed.: Romanticism # HR/1387

J. H. HEXTER: Reappraisals in History: *New Views on History and Society in Early Modern Europe* ° TB/1100

STANLEY HOFFMANN et al.: In Search of France: *The Economy, Society and Political System In the Twentieth Century* TB/1219

H. STUART HUGHES: The Obstructed Path: *French Social Thought in the Years of Desperation* TB/1451

JOHAN HUIZINGA: Dutch Civilisation in the 17th Century and Other Essays TB/1453

LIONAL KOCHAN: The Struggle for Germany: *1914-45* TB/1304

HANS KOHN: The Mind of Germany: *The Education of a Nation* TB/1204

HANS KOHN, Ed.: The Mind of Modern Russia: *Historical and Political Thought of Russia's Great Age* TB/1065

WALTER LAQUEUR & GEORGE L. MOSSE, Eds.: Education and Social Structure in the 20th Century. ° *Volume 6 of the Journal of Contemporary History* TB/1339

WALTER LAQUEUR & GEORGE L. MOSSE, Ed.: International Fascism, 1920-1945. ° *Volume 1 of the Journal of Contemporary History*
TB/1276

WALTER LAQUEUR & GEORGE L. MOSSE, Eds.: Literature and Politics in the 20th Century. ° *Volume 5 of the Journal of Contemporary History.* TB/1328

WALTER LAQUEUR & GEORGE L. MOSSE, Eds.: The New History: *Trends in Historical Research and Writing Since World War II.* ° *Volume 4 of the Journal of Contemporary History*
TB/1327

WALTER LAQUEUR & GEORGE L. MOSSE, Eds.: 1914: *The Coming of the First World War.* ° *Volume3 of the Journal of Contemporary History* TB/1306

C. A. MACARTNEY, Ed.: The Habsburg and Hohenzollern Dynasties in the Seventeenth and Eighteenth Centuries # HR/1400

JOHN MCMANNERS: European History, 1789-1914: *Men, Machines and Freedom* TB/1419

PAUL MANTOUX: The Industrial Revolution in the Eighteenth Century: *An Outline of the Beginnings of the Modern Factory System in England* TB/1079

FRANK E. MANUEL: The Prophets of Paris: *Turgot, Condorcet, Saint-Simon, Fourier, and Comte* TB/1218

KINGSLEY MARTIN: French Liberal Thought in the Eighteenth Century: *A Study of Political Ideas from Bayle to Condorcet* TB/1114

NAPOLEON III: Napoleonic Ideas: *Des Idées Napoléoniennes, par le Prince Napoléon-Louis Bonaparte. Ed. by Brison D. Gooch* ¶
TB/1336

FRANZ NEUMANN: Behemoth: *The Structure and Practice of National Socialism, 1933-1944*
TB/1289

DAVID OGG: Europe of the Ancien Régime, 1715-1783 ° *a* TB/1271

GEORGE RUDE: Revolutionary Europe, 1783-1815 ° *a* TB/1272

MASSIMO SALVADORI, Ed.: Modern Socialism #
TB/1374

HUGH SETON-WATSON: Eastern Europe Between the Wars, 1918-1941 TB/1330

DENIS MACK SMITH, Ed.: The Making of Italy, 1796-1870 # HR/1356

ALBERT SOREL: Europe Under the Old Regime. *Translated by Francis H. Herrick* TB/1121

ROLAND N. STROMBERG, Ed.: Realism, Naturalism, and Symbolism: *Modes of Thought and Expression in Europe, 1848-1914* # HR/1355

A. J. P. TAYLOR: From Napoleon to Lenin: *Historical Essays* ° TB/1268

A. J. P. TAYLOR: The Habsburg Monarchy, 1809-1918: *A History of the Austrian Empire and Austria-Hungary* ° TB/1187

J. M. THOMPSON: European History, 1494-1789
TB/1431

DAVID THOMSON, Ed.: France: Empire and Republic, 1850-1940 # HR/1387

ALEXIS DE TOCQUEVILLE & GUSTAVE DE BEAUMONT: Tocqueville and Beaumont on Social Reform. *Ed. and trans. with Intro. by Seymour Drescher* TB/1343

G. M. TREVELYAN: British History in the Nineteenth Century and After: 1792-1919 °
TB/1251

H. R. TREVOR-ROPER: Historical Essays TB/1269

W. WARREN WAGAR, Ed.: Science, Faith, and MAN: *European Thought Since 1914* #
HR/1362

MACK WALKER, Ed.: Metternich's Europe, 1813-1848 # HR/1361

ELIZABETH WISKEMANN: Europe of the Dictators, 1919-1945 ° *a* TB/1273

JOHN B. WOLF: France: 1814-1919: *The Rise of a Liberal-Democratic Society* TB/3019

Literature & Literary Criticism

JACQUES BARZUN: The House of Intellect
TB/1051

W. J. BATE: From Classic to Romantic: *Premises of Taste in Eighteenth Century England* TB/1036

VAN WYCK BROOKS: Van Wyck Brooks: *The Early Years: A Selection from his Works, 1908-1921* Ed. with Intro. by Claire Sprague TB/3082

ERNST R. CURTIUS: European Literature and the Latin Middle Ages. *Trans. by Willard Trask* TB/2015

RICHMOND LATTIMORE, Translator: The Odyssey of Homer TB/1389

JOHN STUART MILL: On Bentham and Coleridge. *Introduction by F. R. Leavis* TB/1070

SAMUEL PEPYS: The Diary of Samual Pepys. ° *Edited by O. F. Morshead. 60 illus. by Ernest Shepard* TB/1007

ROBERT PREYER, Ed.: Victorian Literature ** TB/1302

ALBION W. TOURGEE: A Fool's Errand: *A Novel of the South during Reconstruction. Intro. by George Fredrickson* TB/3074

BASIL WILEY: Nineteenth Century Studies: *Coleridge to Matthew Arnold* ° TB/1261

RAYMOND WILLIAMS: Culture and Society, 1780-1950 ° TB/1252

Philosophy

HENRI BERGSON: Time and Free Will: *An Essay on the Immediate Data of Consciousness* ° TB/1021

LUDWIG BINSWANGER: Being-in-the-World: *Selected Papers. Trans. with Intro. by Jacob Needleman* TB/1365

H. J. BLACKHAM: Six Existentialist Thinkers: *Kierkegaard, Nietzsche, Jaspers, Marcel, Heidegger, Sartre* ° TB/1002

J. M. BOCHENSKI: The Methods of Contemporary Thought. *Trans. by Peter Caws* TB/1377

CRANE BRINTON: Nietzsche. *Preface, Bibliography, and Epilogue by the Author* TB/1197

ERNST CASSIRER: Rousseau, Kant and Goethe. *Intro. by Peter Gay* TB/1092

FREDERICK COPLESTON, S. J.: Medieval Philosophy TB/376

F. M. CORNFORD: From Religion to Philosophy: *A Study in the Origins of Western Speculation* § TB/20

WILFRID DESAN: The Tragic Finale: *An Essay on the Philosophy of Jean-Paul Sartre* TB/1030

MARVIN FARBER: The Aims of Phenomenology: *The Motives, Methods, and Impact of Husserl's Thought* TB/1291

MARVIN FARBER: Basic Issues of Philosophy: *Experience, Reality, and Human Values* TB/1344

MARVIN FARBER: Phenomenology and Existence: *Towards a Philosophy within Nature* TB/1295

PAUL FRIEDLANDER: Plato: *An Introduction* TB/2017

MICHAEL GELVEN: A Commentary on Heidegger's "Being and Time" TB/1464

J. GLENN GRAY: Hegel and Greek Thought TB/1409

W. K. C. GUTHRIE: The Greek Philosophers: *From Thales to Aristotle* ° TB/1008

G. W. F. HEGEL: On Art, Religion Philosophy: *Introductory Lectures to the Realm of Absolute Spirit.* || *Edited with an Introduction by J. Glenn Gray* TB/1463

G. W. F. HEGEL: Phenomenology of Mind. ° || *Introduction by George Lichtheim* TB/1303

MARTIN HEIDEGGER: Discourse on Thinking. *Translated with a Preface by John M. Anderson and E. Hans Freund. Introduction by John M. Anderson* TB/1459

F. H. HEINEMANN: Existentialism and the Modern Predicament TB/28

WERER HEISENBERG: Physics and Philosophy: *The Revolution in Modern Science. Intro. by F. S. C. Northrop* TB/549

EDMUND HUSSERL: Phenomenology and the Crisis of Philosophy. § *Translated with an Introduction by Quentin Lauer* TB/1170

IMMANUEL KANT: Groundwork of the Metaphysic of Morals. *Translated and Analyzed by H. J. Paton* TB/1159

IMMANUEL KANT: Lectures on Ethics. § *Introduction by Lewis White Beck* TB/105

WALTER KAUFMANN, Ed.: Religion From Tolstoy to Camus: *Basic Writings on Religious Truth and Morals* TB/123

QUENTIN LAUER: Phenomenology: *Its Genesis and Prospect. Preface by Aron Gurwitsch* TB/1169

MAURICE MANDELBAUM: The Problem of Historical Knowledge: *An Answer to Relativism* TB/1338

GEORGE A. MORGAN: What Nietzsche Means TB/1198

H. J. PATON: The Categorical Imperative: *A Study in Kant's Moral Philosophy* TB/1325

MICHAEL POLANYI: Personal Knowledge: *Towards a Post-Critical Philosophy* TB/1158

KARL R. POPPER: Conjectures and Refutations: *The Growth of Scientific Knowledge* TB/1376

WILLARD VAN ORMAN QUINE: Elementary Logic *Revised Edition* TB/577

WILLARD VAN ORMAN QUINE: From a Logical Point of View: *Logico-Philosophical Essays* TB/566

JOHN E. SMITH: Themes in American Philosophy: *Purpose, Experience and Community* TB/1466

MORTON WHITE: Foundations of Historical Knowledge TB/1440

WILHELM WINDELBAND: A History of Philosophy *Vol. I: Greek, Roman, Medieval* TB/38 *Vol. II; Renaissance, Enlightenment, Modern* TB/39

LUDWIG WITTGENSTEIN: The Blue and Brown Books ° TB/1211

LUDWIG WITTGENSTEIN: Notebooks, 1914-1916 TB/1441

Political Science & Government

C. E. BLACK: The Dynamics of Modernization: *A Study in Comparative History* TB/1321

KENNETH E. BOULDING: Conflict and Defense: *A General Theory of Action* TB/3024

DENIS W. BROGAN: Politics in America. *New Introduction by the Author* TB/1469

CRANE BRINTON: English Political Thought in the Nineteenth Century TB/1071

ROBERT CONQUEST: Power and Policy in the USSR: *The Study of Soviet Dynastics* ° TB/1307

ROBERT A. DAHL & CHARLES E. LINDBLOM: Politics, Economics, and Welfare: *Planning and Politico-Economic Systems Resolved into Basic Social Processes* TB/1277

HANS KOHN: Political Ideologies of the 20th Century TB/1277

ROY C. MACRIDIS, Ed.: Political Parties: *Contemporary Trends and Ideas* ** TB/1322

ROBERT GREEN MC CLOSKEY: American Conservatism in the Age of Enterprise, 1865-1910 TB/1137

MARSILIUS OF PADUA: The Defender of Peace. The Defensor Pacis. *Translated with an Introduction by Alan Gewirth* TB/1310

KINGSLEY MARTIN: French Liberal Thought in the Eighteenth Century: *A Study of Political Ideas from Bayle to Condorcet* TB/1114

BARRINGTON MOORE, JR.: Political Power and Social Theory: *Seven Studies* || TB/1221

BARRINGTON MOORE, JR.: Soviet Politics—The Dilemma of Power: *The Role of Ideas in Social Change* || TB/1222

BARRINGTON MOORE, JR.: Terror and Progress—USSR: *Some Sources of Change and Stability*

JOHN B. MORRALL: Political Thought in Medieval Times TB/1076

KARL R. POPPER: The Open Society and Its Enemies *Vol. I: The Spell of Plato* TB/1101 *Vol. II: The High Tide of Prophecy: Hegel, Marx, and the Aftermath* TB/1102

CONYERS READ, Ed.: The Constitution Reconsidered. *Revised Edition, Preface by Richard B. Morris* TB/1384

JOHN P. ROCHE, Ed.: Origins of American Political Thought: *Selected Readings* TB/1301

JOHN P. ROCHE, Ed.: American Political Thought: *From Jefferson to Progressivism* TB/1332

HENRI DE SAINT-SIMON: Social Organization, The Science of Man, and Other Writings. || *Edited and Translated with an Introduction by Felix Markham* TB/1152

CHARLES SCHOTTLAND, Ed.: The Welfare State ** TB/1323

JOSEPH A. SCHUMPETER: Capitalism, Socialism and Democracy TB/3008

PETER WOLL, Ed.: Public Administration and Policy: *Selected Essays* TB/1284

Psychology

ALFRED ADLER: The Individual Psychology of Alfred Adler: *A Systematic Presentation in Selections from His Writings. Edited by Heinz L. & Rowena R. Ansbacher* TB/1154

ALFRED ADLER: Problems of Neurosis: *A Book of Case Histories. Introduction by Heinz L. Ansbacher* TB/1145

LUDWIG BINSWANGER: Being-in-the-World: *Selected Papers. || Trans. with Intro. by Jacob Needleman* TB/1365

ARTHUR BURTON & ROBERT E. HARRIS: Clinical Studies of Personality Vol. I TB/3075 Vol. II TB/3076

HADLEY CANTRIL: The Invasion from Mars: *A Study in the Psychology of Panic* || TB/1282

MIRCEA ELIADE: Cosmos and History: *The Myth of the Eternal Return* § TB/2050

MIRCEA ELIADE: Myth and Reality TB/1369

MIRCEA ELIADE: Myths, Dreams and Mysteries: *The Encounter Between Contemporary Faiths and Archaic Realities* § TB/1320

MIRCEA ELIADE: Rites and Symbols of Initiation: *The Mysteries of Birth and Rebirth* § TB/1236

HERBERT FINGARETTE: The Self in Transformation: *Psychoanalysis, Philosophy and the Life of the Spirit* || TB/1177

SIGMUND FREUD: On Creativity and the Unconscious: *Papers on the Psychology of Art, Literature, Love, Religion. § Intro. by Benjamin Nelson* TB/45

J. GLENN GRAY: The Warriors: *Reflections on Men in Battle. Introduction by Hannah Arendt* TB/1294

WILLIAM JAMES: Psychology: *The Briefer Course. Edited with an Intro. by Gordon Allport* TB/1034

C. G. JUNG: Psychological Reflections. *Ed. by J. Jacobi* TB/2001

KARL MENNINGER, M.D.: Theory of Psychoanalytic Technique TB/1144

JOHN H. SCHAAR: Escape from Authority: *The Perspectives of Erich Fromm* TB/1155

MUZAFER SHERIF: The Psychology of Social Norms. *Introduction by Gardner Murphy* TB/3072

HELLMUT WILHELM: Change: *Eight Lectures on the I Ching* TB/2019

Religion: Ancient and Classical, Biblical and Judaic Traditions

W. F. ALBRIGHT: The Biblical Period from Abraham to Ezra TB/102

SALO W. BARON: Modern Nationalism and Religion TB/818

C. K. BARRETT, Ed.: The New Testament Background: *Selected Documents* TB/86

MARTIN BUBER: Eclipse of God: *Studies in the Relation Between Religion and Philosophy* TB/12

MARTIN BUBER: Hasidism and Modern Man. *Edited and Translated by Maurice Friedman* TB/839

MARTIN BUBER: The Knowledge of Man. *Edited with an Introduction by Maurice Friedman. Translated by Maurice Friedman and Ronald Gregor Smith* TB/135

MARTIN BUBER: Moses. *The Revelation and the Covenant* TB/837

MARTIN BUBER: The Origin and Meaning of Hasidism. *Edited and Translated by Maurice Friedman* TB/835

MARTIN BUBER: The Prophetic Faith TB/73

MARTIN BUBER: Two Types of Faith: *Interpenetration of Judaism and Christianity* ° TB/75

MALCOLM L. DIAMOND: Martin Buber: *Jewish Existentialist* TB/840

M. S. ENSLIN: Christian Beginnings TB/5

M. S. ENSLIN: The Literature of the Christian Movement TB/6

ERNST LUDWIG EHRLICH: A Concise History of Israel: *From the Earliest Times to the Destruction of the Temple in A.D. 70* ° TB/128

HENRI FRANKFORT: Ancient Egyptian Religion: *An Interpretation* TB/77

MAURICE S. FRIEDMAN: Martin Buber: *The Life of Dialogue* TB/64

ABRAHAM HESCHEL: The Earth Is the Lord's & The Sabbath. *Two Essays* TB/828

ABRAHAM HESCHEL: God in Search of Man: *A Philosophy of Judaism* TB/807

ABRAHAM HESCHEL: Man Is not Alone: *A Philosophy of Religion* TB/838

ABRAHAM HESCHEL: The Prophets: *An Introduction* TB/1421

T. J. MEEK: Hebrew Origins TB/69

JAMES MUILENBURG: The Way of Israel: *Biblical Faith and Ethics* TB/133

H. J. ROSE: Religion in Greece and Rome TB/55

H. H. ROWLEY: The Growth of the Old Testament TB/107

D. WINTON THOMAS, Ed.: Documents from Old Testament Times TB/85

Religion: General Christianity

ROLAND H. BAINTON: Christendom: *A Short History of Christianity and Its Impact on Western Civilization. Illus.* Vol. I TB/131; Vol. II TB/132

JOHN T. MCNEILL: Modern Christian Movements. *Revised Edition* TB/1402

ERNST TROELTSCH: The Social Teaching of the Christian Churches. *Intro. by H. Richard Niebuhr* Vol. TB/71; Vol. II TB/72

Religion: Early Christianity Through Reformation

ANSELM OF CANTERBURY: Truth, Freedom, and Evil: *Three Philosophical Dialogues. Edited and Translated by Jasper Hopkins and Herbert Richardson* TB/317

MARSHALL W. BALDWIN, Ed.: Christianity through the 13th Century # HR/1468

W. D. DAVIES: Paul and Rabbinic Judaism: *Some Rabbinic Elements in Pauline Theology. Revised Edition* ° TB/146

ADOLF DEISSMAN: Paul: *A Study in Social and Religious History* TB/15

JOHANNES ECKHART: Meister Eckhart: *A Modern Translation by R. Blakney* TB/8

EDGAR J. GOODSPEED: A Life of Jesus TB/1

ROBERT M. GRANT: Gnosticism and Early Christianity TB/136

WILLIAM HALLER: The Rise of Puritanism TB/22

GERHART B. LADNER: The Idea of Reform: *Its Impact on the Christian Thought and Action in the Age of the Fathers* TB/149

ARTHUR DARBY NOCK: Early Gentile Christianity and Its Hellenistic Background TB/111

ARTHUR DARBY NOCK: St. Paul ° TB/104

ORIGEN: On First Principles. *Edited by G. W. Butterworth. Introduction by Henri de Lubac* TB/311

GORDON RUPP: Luther's Progress to the Diet of Worms ° TB/120

Religion: The Protestant Tradition

KARL BARTH: Church Dogmatics: *A Selection. Intro. by H. Gollwitzer. Ed. by G. W. Bromiley* TB/95

KARL BARTH: Dogmatics in Outline TB/56

KARL BARTH: The Word of God and the Word of Man TB/13

HERBERT BRAUN, et al.: God and Christ: *Existence and Province. Volume 5 of* Journal for Theology and the Church, *edited by Robert W. Funk and Gerhard Ebeling* TB/255

WHITNEY R. CROSS: The Burned-Over District: *The Social and Intellectual History of Enthusiastic Religion in Western New York, 1800-1850* TB/1242

NELS F. S. FERRE: Swedish Contributions to Modern Theology. *New Chapter by William A. Johnson* TB/147

WILLIAM R. HUTCHISON, Ed.: American Protestant Thought: *The Liberal Era* † TB/1385

ERNST KASEMANN, et al.: Distinctive Protestant and Catholic Themes Reconsidered. *Volume 3 of* Journal for Theology and the Church, *edited by Robert W. Funk and Gerhard Ebeling* TB/253

SOREN KIERKEGAARD: On Authority and Revelation: *The Book on Adler, or a Cycle of Ethico-Religious Essays. Introduction by F. Sontag* TB/139

SOREN KIERKEGAARD: Crisis in the Life of an Actress, *and Other Essays on Drama. Translated with an Introduction by Stephen Crites* TB/145

SOREN KIERKEGAARD: Edifying Discourses. *Edited with an Intro. by Paul Holmer* TB/32

SOREN KIERKEGAARD: The Journals of Kierkegaard. ° *Edited with an Intro. by Alexander Dru* TB/52

SOREN KIERKEGAARD: The Point of View for My Work as an Author: *A Report to History.* § *Preface by Benjamin Nelson* TB/88

SOREN KIERKEGAARD: The Present Age. § *Translated and edited by Alexander Dru. Introduction by Walter Kaufmann* TB/94

SOREN KIERKEGAARD: Purity of Heart. *Trans. by Douglas Steere* TB/4

SOREN KIERKEGAARD: Repetition: *An Essay in Experimental Psychology* § TB/117

SOREN KIERKEGAARD: Works of Love: *Some Christian Reflections in the Form of Discourses* TB/122

WILLIAM G. MCLOUGHLIN, Ed.: The American Evangelicals: 1800-1900: *An Anthology* TB/1382

WOLFHART PANNENBERG, et al.: History and Hermeneutic. *Volume 4 of* Journal for Theology and the Church, *edited by Robert W. Funk and Gerhard Ebeling* TB/254

JAMES M. ROBINSON, et al.: The Bultmann School of Biblical Interpretation: New Directions? *Volume 1 of* Journal for Theology and the Church, *edited by Robert W. Funk and Gerhard Ebeling* TB/251

F. SCHLEIERMACHER: The Christian Faith. *Introduction by Richard R. Niebuhr.* Vol. I TB/108; Vol. II TB/109

F. SCHLEIERMACHER: On Religion: *Speeches to Its Cultured Despisers. Intro. by Rudolf Otto* TB/36

TIMOTHY L. SMITH: Revivalism and Social Reform: *American Protestantism on the Eve of the Civil War* TB/1229

PAUL TILLICH: Dynamics of Faith TB/42

PAUL TILLICH: Morality and Beyond TB/142

EVELYN UNDERHILL: Worship TB/10

Religion: The Roman & Eastern Christian Traditions

A. ROBERT CAPONIGRI, Ed.: Modern Catholic Thinkers II: *The Church and the Political Order* TB/307

G. P. FEDOTOV: The Russian Religious Mind: *Kievan Christianity, the tenth to the thirteenth Centuries* TB/370

GABRIEL MARCEL: Being and Having: *An Existential Diary. Introduction by James Collins* TB/310

GABRIEL MARCEL: Homo Viator: *Introduction to a Metaphysic of Hope* TB/397

Religion: Oriental Religions

TOR ANDRAE: Mohammed: *The Man and His Faith* § TB/62

EDWARD CONZE: Buddhism: *Its Essence and Development.* ° *Foreword by Arthur Waley* TB/58

EDWARD CONZE: Buddhist Meditation TB/1442

EDWARD CONZE et al, Editors: Buddhist Texts through the Ages TB/113

ANANDA COOMARASWAMY: Buddha and the Gospel of Buddhism TB/119

H. G. CREEL: Confucius and the Chinese Way TB/63

FRANKLIN EDGERTON, Trans. & Ed.: The Bhagavad Gita TB/115

SWAMI NIKHILANANDA, Trans. & Ed.: The Upanishads TB/114

D. T. SUZUKI: On Indian Mahayana Buddhism. ° *Ed. with Intro. by Edward Conze.* TB/1403

Religion: Philosophy, Culture, and Society

NICOLAS BERDYAEV: The Destiny of Man TB/61

RUDOLF BULTMANN: History and Eschatology: *The Presence of Eternity* ° TB/91

RUDOLF BULTMANN AND FIVE CRITICS: Kerygma and Myth: *A Theological Debate* TB/80

9

RUDOLF BULTMANN and KARL KUNDSIN: Form Criticism: *Two Essays on New Testament Research. Trans. by F. C. Grant* TB/96
WILLIAM A. CLEBSCH & CHARLES R. JAEKLE: Pastoral Care in Historical Perspective: *An Essay with Exhibits* TB/148
FREDERICK FERRE: Language, Logic and God. *New Preface by the Author* TB/1407
LUDWIG FEUERBACH: The Essence of Christianity. § *Introduction by Karl Barth. Foreword by H. Richard Niebuhr* TB/11
C. C. GILLISPIE: Genesis and Geology: *The Decades before Darwin* § TB/51
ADOLF HARNACK: What Is Christianity? § *Introduction by Rudolf Bultmann* TB/17
KYLE HASELDEN: The Racial Problem in Christian Perspective TB/116
MARTIN HEIDEGGER: Discourse on Thinking. *Translated with a Preface by John M. Anderson and E. Hans Freund. Introduction by John M. Anderson* TB/1459
IMMANUEL KANT: Religion Within the Limits of Reason Alone. § *Introduction by Theodore M. Greene and John Silber* TB/FG
WALTER KAUFMANN, Ed.: Religion from Tolstoy to Camus: *Basic Writings on Religious Truth and Morals. Enlarged Edition* TB/123
JOHN MACQUARRIE: An Existentialist Theology: *A Comparison of Heidegger and Bultmann. ° Foreword by Rudolf Bultmann* TB/125
H. RICHARD NIERUHR: Christ and Culture TB/3
H. RICHARD NIEBUHR: The Kingdom of God in America TB/49
ANDERS NYGREN: Agape and Eros. *Translated by Philip S. Watson* ° TB/1430
JOHN H. RANDALL, JR.: The Meaning of Religion for Man. *Revised with New Intro. by the Author* TB/1379
WALTER RAUSCHENBUSCHS Christianity and the Social Crisis. ‡ *Edited by Robert D. Cross* TB/3059
JOACHIM WACH: Understanding and Believing. *Ed. with Intro. by Joseph M. Kitagawa* TB/1399

Science and Mathematics

JOHN TYLER BONNER: The Ideas of Biology. Σ *Illus.* TB/570
W. E. LE GROS CLARK: The Antecedents of Man: *An Introduction to the Evolution of the Primates.* ° *Illus.* TB/559
ROBERT E. COKER: Streams, Lakes, Ponds. *Illus.* TB/586
ROBERT E. COKER: This Great and Wide Sea: *An Introduction to Oceanography and Marine Biology. Illus.* TB/551
W. H. DOWDESWELL: Animal Ecology. *61 illus.* TB/543
C. V. DURELL: Readable Relativity. *Foreword by Freeman J. Dyson* TB/530
GEORGE GAMOW: Biography of Physics. Σ *Illus.* TB/567
F. K. HARE: The Restless Atmosphere TB/560
S. KORNER: The Philosophy of Mathematics: *An Introduction* TB/547
J. R. PIERCE: Symbols, Signals and Noise: *The Nature and Process of Communication* Σ TB/574
WILLARD VAN ORMAN QUINE: Mathematical Logic TB/558

Science: History

MARIE BOAS: The Scientific Renaissance, 1450-1630 ° TB/583
W. DAMPIER, Ed.: Readings in the Literature of Science. *Illus.* TB/512

STEPHEN TOULMIN & JUNE GOODFIELD: The Architecture of Matter: *The Physics, Chemistry and Physiology of Matter, Both Animate and Inanimate, as it has Evolved since the Beginnings of Science* TB/584
STEPHEN TOULMIN & JUNE GOODFIELD: The Discovery of Time TB/585
STEPHEN TOULMIN & JUNE GOODFIELD: The Fabric of the Heavens: *The Development of Astronomy and Dynamics* TB/579

Science: Philosophy

J. M. BOCHENSKI: The Methods of Contemporary Thought. *Tr. by Peter Caws* TB/1377
J. BRONOWSKI: Science and Human Values. *Revised and Enlarged. Illus.* TB/505
WERNER HEISENBERG: Physics and Philosophy: *The Revolution in Modern Science. Introduction by F. S. C. Northrop* TB/549
KARL R. POPPER: Conjectures and Refutations: *The Growth of Scientific Knowledge* TB/1376
KARL R. POPPER: The Logic of Scientific Discovery TB/576
STEPHEN TOULMIN: Foresight and Understanding: *An Enquiry into the Aims of Science. Foreword by Jacques Barzun* TB/564
STEPHEN TOULMIN: The Philosophy of Science: *An Introduction* TB/513

Sociology and Anthropology

REINHARD BENDIX: Work and Authority in Industry: *Ideologies of Management in the Course of Industrialization* TB/3035
BERNARD BERELSON, Ed., The Behavioral Sciences Today TB/1127
JOSEPH B. CASAGRANDE, Ed.: In the Company of Man: *Twenty Portraits of Anthropological Informants. Illus.* TB/3047
KENNETH B. CLARK: Dark Ghetto: *Dilemmas of Social Power. Foreword by Gunnar Myrdal* TB/1317
KENNETH CLARK & JEANNETTE HOPKINS: A Relevant War Against Poverty: *A Study of Community Action Programs and Observable Social Change* TB/1480
W. E. LE GROS CLARK: The Antecedents of Man: *An Introduction to the Evolution of the Primates.* ° *Illus.* TB/559
LEWIS COSER, Ed.: Political Sociology TB/1293
ROSE L. COSER, Ed.: Life Cycle and Achievement in America ** TB/1434
ALLISON DAVIS & JOHN DOLLARD: Children of Bondage: *The Personality Development of Negro Youth in the Urban South* || TB/3049
ST. CLAIR DRAKE & HORACE R. CAYTON: Black Metropolis: *A Study of Negro Life in a Northern City. Introduction by Everett C. Hughes. Tables, maps, charts, and graphs* Vol. I TB/1086; Vol. II TB/1087
PETER E. DRUCKER: The New Society: *The Anatomy of Industrial Order* TB/1082
CORA DU BOIS: The People of Alor. *With a Preface by the Author* Vol. I *Illus.* TB/1042; Vol. II TB/1043
EMILE DURKHEIM et al.: Essays on Sociology and Philosophy: *with Appraisals of Durkheim's Life and Thought.* || *Edited by Kurt H. Wolff* TB/1151
LEON FESTINGER, HENRY W. RIECKEN, STANLEY SCHACHTER: When Prophecy Fails: *A Social and Psychological Study of a Modern Group that Predicted the Destruction of the World* || TB/1132

10

CHARLES Y. GLOCK & RODNEY STARK: Christian Beliefs and Anti-Semitism. *Introduction by the Authors* TB/1454

ALVIN W. GOULDNER: The Hellenic World TB/1479

ALVIN W. GOULDNER: Wildcat Strike: *A Study in Worker-Management Relationships* || TB/1176

CESAR GRANA: Modernity and Its Discontents: *French Society and the French Man of Letters in the Nineteenth Century* TB/1318

L. S. B. LEAKEY: Adam's Ancestors: *The Evolution of Man and His Culture. Illus.* TB/1019

KURT LEWIN: Field Theory in Social Science: *Selected Theoretical Papers.* || *Edited by Dorwin Cartwright* TB/1135

RITCHIE P. LOWRY: Who's Running This Town? *Community Leadership and Social Change* TB/1383

R. M. MACIVER: Social Causation TB/1153

GARY T. MARX: Protest and Prejudice: *A Study of Belief in the Black Community* TB/1435

ROBERT K. MERTON, LEONARD BROOM, LEONARD S. COTTRELL, JR., Editors: Sociology Today: *Problems and Prospects* || Vol. I TB/1173; Vol. II TB/1174

GILBERT OSOFSKY, Ed.: The Burden of Race: *A Documentary History of Negro-White Relations in America* TB/1405

GILBERT OSOFSKY: Harlem: The Making of a Ghetto: *Negro New York 1890-1930* TB/1381

TALCOTT PARSONS & EDWARD A. SHILS, Editors: Toward a General Theory of Action: *Theoretical Foundations for the Social Sciences* TB/1083

PHILIP RIEFF: The Triumph of the Therapeutic: *Uses of Faith After Freud* TB/1360

JOHN H. ROHRER & MUNRO S. EDMONSON, Eds.: The Eighth Generation Grows Up: *Cultures and Personalities of New Orleans Negroes* || TB/3050

ARNOLD ROSE: The Negro in America: *The Condensed Version of Gunnar Myrdal's* An American Dilemma. *Second Edition* TB/3048

GEORGE ROSEN: Madness in Society: *Chapters in the Historical Sociology of Mental Illness.* || *Preface by Benjamin Nelson* TB/1337

PHILIP SELZNICK: TVA and the Grass Roots: *A Study in the Sociology of Formal Organization* TB/1230

PITIRIM A. SOROKIN: Contemporary Sociological Theories: *Through the First Quarter of the Twentieth Century* TB/3046

MAURICE R. STEIN: The Eclipse of Community: *An Interpretation of American Studies* TB/1128

WILLIAM I. THOMAS: The Unadjusted Girl: *With Cases and Standpoint for Behavior Analysis. Intro. by Michael Parenti* TB/1319

EDWARD A. TIRYAKIAN, Ed.: Sociological Theory, Values and Sociocultural Change: *Essays in Honor of Pitirim A. Sorokin* ° TB/1316

FERDINAND TONNIES: Community and Society: *Gemeinschaft und Gesellschaft. Translated and Edited by Charles P. Loomis* TB/1116

SAMUEL E. WALLACE: Skid Row as a Way of Life TB/1367

W. LLOYD WARNER and Associates: Democracy in Jonesville: *A Study in Quality and Inequality* || TB/1129

W. LLOYD WARNER: Social Class in America: *The Evaluation of Status* TB/1013

FLORIAN ZNANIECKI: The Social Role of the Man of Knowledge. *Introduction by Lewis A. Coser* TB/1372